# Rudi of the Mountains

RUD

FR

# of the Mountains

## ROBERT RECHER

Translated by
### HELEN RAMSBOTHAM

Illustrated by
### REG S. GRAY

CRITERION BOOKS · NEW YORK

*21,844*

*303*

First American edition published by
Criterion Books, Inc. 1965

First edition in the United Kingdom
© translation Oliver & Boyd Ltd.1964

Library of Congress Catalog
Card Number: 65-23589

First published in France as
"Rudi et le Chamois"
by Editions de l'Amitié, G. T. Rageot


Printed in the United States of America

# Contents

The mountain heights are given in metres. One
metre is a little more than 3 feet (39·37 inches.)

# 1

## Peter's Mountains

' Hi there, Larry—are you still dreaming ? '

' Umm ?  Of course not !  I was just thinking what fun it is to see the village so far down below us, as if we were in an aeroplane ; it's like looking at a map.'

' Just what I thought—day-dreaming again ! '

The two boys were lying flat out in the lush grass at the very edge of the sloping mountain pasture (see map on page 63), just where it broke off sheer to overhang the valley at a giddy height.  Their heads jutted out over the projecting ridge, and to imagine themselves suspended in space over the abyss, while knowing that they were perfectly safe all the time, gave them a delicious thrill of fear.

They had stopped to rest here on their way home from an afternoon's long tramp—two sturdy fourteen-year-olds : Larry from the city, who had rather outgrown his strength, but was full of life and spirits and very highly strung, although given to day-dreaming ; and his friend Peter, who was a true mountain-dweller, slow but sure in all his movements.

' You know,' said Larry, ' although it's five years now since my parents started renting your house for the holidays while you and your family took the animals higher up the mountain, this is the first time I've really enjoyed myself. Perhaps I was too young before —I don't know—but I can't tell you how thrilled I was to get to Kandersteg this year ! I think it's probably because it was fixed that I should spend my holidays high on the mountain with you. It's so different up here ! We're as free as air—and it's absolutely grand.'

' Yes, you really didn't know much about the mountains before—you'd only been on a few trips, which hardly counted. I must say they're terrific—just look at that ! '

Opposite them, on the other side of the narrow steep-sided valley, rose the magnificent Blümlisalp with its glaciers like petrified torrents, its sparkling masses of frozen snow and its rocky peaks outlined against the clear blue sky. It was a world of silence and icy solitude whose beauty and serenity dominated the surrounding countryside.

Peter had told his friend the names of all the peaks and had shown him where all the mountain huts stood. He was never tired of talking about *his* mountains, and could go on describing them for hours—the pine and larch plantations covering the steep slopes, the green mountain pastures, Fisi's ornamental turret-like peaks and the Doldenhorn's huge slabs. To the

8

left lay the Schneehorn's clear-cut snow cornice, glistening in the sunshine, the sheer walls of the Rothorn and the Blümlisalp's dazzling peaks.

' Isn't it glorious ? '

' I should say so ! Things look quite different up here—it's another world altogether from the view you can see from the valley. It's wonderful, you feel that you are right at the heart of the mountain ! '

' Now it's time to get going again,' said Peter. ' We mustn't stay here too long—it'll take us nearly two hours to get back to the chalet.'

' Do just wait a minute—it's so perfect here ! '

' That's all very well—what'll happen if we're too late to fetch the cows in ? '

Peter took a running leap at his friend, dragged him backwards and began pummelling him, calling out :

' Lazy-bones, lazy-bones ! '

They wrestled for a moment or two, rolling over and over in the grass, seizing each other round the waist and guffawing with laughter, till Larry called out for mercy. ' Stop it—you're suffocating me ! '

Peter didn't give up, however, until Larry had promised to bring in the herd ; then he dashed off as fast as he could down the mountain, yodelling gaily. Larry just had to follow him, and got out of breath trying to catch up.

Peter, like a true mountaineer, was quite tireless, and he could slog on for hours at the same steady pace, however steep or difficult the going, without showing any signs of fatigue except that his breath came more rapidly, whereas Larry, who spent only one month a year in the mountains, was hard put to it to keep up. Peter, however, had thought out a way of breaking his friend into things gently. For the first few days all they did was to explore the Golitschenalp pastures surrounding their chalet, gradually extending their field of operations and climbing up to the col or pass at the foot of the pyramid called First, which took them over to the Almenalp ; here they visited old Harry in his little hut, isolated like their own in the midst of the mountains. Then they explored the entrances to the huge *couloirs* or gullies of the Almengrat, hunting for the lovely veined stones to be found there and finding rock crystal too if they were lucky. They had even made a rash attempt to scale the lower slopes of the Lohner peaks. ' After all,' said Peter, ' we're tough, and it's not as dangerous as all that ! '

Larry was thrilled with everything—the freedom of their life in the mountains, which seemed to belong only to them ; having Peter, with all his strength and generosity, as a friend, indeed almost a brother ; and the whole magnificent panorama of the Bernese Oberland with which they were surrounded. His one ambition was to climb higher and higher—all he thought of was crossing glaciers and frozen snow, and scaling rocks.

' Shall we go over the col again coming back ? '
asked Larry.

' Yes, I suppose so—wait a minute though—we
could go home a different way and have some fun—
listen ! '

The two boys came to a standstill, and Peter began
explaining, pointing as he did so.

' Do you see the col and the Golitschengrat ridge
leading down from it ?  First of all there are those
funny little *gendarme* rocks, then some like jagged
teeth, and then the ridge seems to straighten out,
doesn't it ? '

' Yes—almost like a little platform.'

' Well, we're going to climb up there and . . .'

' Are you kidding ?  It's as steep as anything ! '

' We're not going to climb straight up, you ass !
We'd have to be roped together, and anyway we
couldn't do it.  No, there's a little diagonal path which
will get us there quite easily—you'll see !  It'll save us
nearly an hour and it will be great fun coming down
the mountain on the other side.'

In fact, after scrambling through the rhododendron
bushes at the foot of the slope, they did come upon a
track, leading up through some fallen rocks, which
brought them out on to the little platform after a
quarter of an hour's climb.

At their feet lay the Golitschenalp with its huge
velvety green slopes, which seem to rise against the First

11

peak in successive waves breaking on its rocky spurs, while on the opposite side it dominates the whole valley with a sheer thousand-metre peak.

Larry's breath was completely taken away and for some time he could not speak. He knew the Golitschenalp well, having explored it thoroughly with Peter, but never before had he had such a perfect vision of it as a whole. The immensity of it, the freedom and grandeur of the magnificent landscape, the intoxicating sound of the wind on the mountain top, all went to his head—he was monarch of all he surveyed.

' It's superb ! '

Peter understood exactly how his friend was feeling —deeply moved and tremendously thrilled. He took his arm.

' Yes, it's glorious—I'm so glad you're here. But let's hurry and go down—it isn't too steep, you'll see.'

' What, is this the way we've got to . . .'

' Don't worry,' cut in Peter, ' it's a piece of cake ! We'll climb up again first as far as that fissure there, scramble through and in ten minutes we'll be out on the mountain-side.'

Larry gave a long whistle. ' That's all very fine ! We'll break our necks ! '

' Nonsense ! It isn't as steep as all that—once we get going you'll think nothing of it. Do you see this fissure ? It leads down to the meadow, and as it's so narrow you can hold on to the sides, and slide along on your behind, using your legs as brakes ! It's so jagged that you're sure to find footholds and handholds. Come on, let's go ! Follow me and don't flap ! '

Peter spoke with such authority that Larry simply had to follow him into the narrow gap between the rocks. His heart beat wildly and a lump came into his throat, but the reassuring sight of his friend's mop of fair hair and broad shoulders just below gave him courage. He could trust Peter, who certainly must know this path well and would not have brought him there if it were really dangerous. In any case, he soon forgot the valley below and the loose stones to left and right of him slipping down into its depths. The fissure began to seem like a rough stairway ; it was even possible to sit down or at least prop oneself up against the sides to rest.

Larry soon got the hang of it and began thoroughly to enjoy this new kind of acrobatics. From time to time Peter raised his head to cheer him on, but there was no need : Larry moved with complete assurance, finding the right footholds, no longer feeling his way haphazardly, but gripping with firm hands. Novice that he was, he already felt instinctively the satisfaction of the climber pitting his wits and his strength against the mountain.

' Everything O.K., Larry ? '

' You bet it is ! It's dead easy ! And we're really climbing now ! '

Peter stopped on a wide ledge which cut across the rock-face half-way down and began to laugh.

'That's right, go ahead and fancy yourself as a famous climber! Snap out of it, this is only a tiny little rock, just the size for boys like us, not much higher than the rock in the monkeys' cage at the Basle Zoo.'

'You always exaggerate like mad,' protested Larry, who had joined him.

'Hardly at all! Listen, though, don't tell Father about this all the same. *We* know how easy it is, but if he knew that we did this kind of thing he'd box my ears.'

'Why on earth? Surely he must guess that you do a bit of climbing here and there.'

'Of course he does; besides, we've often been down through this fissure together. It's not that, it's because of you. He'd certainly not approve of your doing this kind of thing—supposing something happened . . .'

'What could happen? There's nothing tricky about it—you've only got to stay the course!'

'Yes, I know, but mind you don't try it out alone; it could be dangerous, and . . .'

'All right—don't preach at me! You know perfectly well that we're always together and I simply follow you.'

'Come on, then, and don't breathe a word tonight.'

They went on with their descent, one above the other

14

all the way, but gathering speed, for the slope grew more pronounced as they drew near the pasture. They were even able to run for the last few yards, and finally flung themselves down on the grass, bursting with laughter.

Larry lay on his back gazing up at *his* fissure.

' I say, Peter, from here it hardly looks anything— but from the top . . .'

' Yes, it's always like that. Coming down seems steeper than going up. It's because you can see the drop beneath, you know.'

' It was great, Peter ! I do hope there's lots more climbing like that to do ! '

Peter, who was gazing at the rock-face, did not reply. He seized Larry's arm abruptly, and pointing over to the right, exclaimed, ' Whoever's that ? '

## 2

## *Rudi Goes Climbing*

Larry drew away instinctively ; he was still in the grip of the emotion caused by his first attempt at real climbing and his friend's rather brutal interruption cut across his golden dreams.

'Why—what's the matter ? '

'Look at those rocks in the shadow—there's someone there ! '

'I can't see anything.  Where ? '

'There *is* someone ;  look at that peak jutting out of the ridge—that big spur cutting across the mountain ! Don't you see ?  About a third of the way up, starting from the bottom.  There's a chap hanging on to the rock-face.  I wonder what he's doing there.'

'Oh yes, I can just make him out, but not very clearly, he's right in the shadow.  You've certainly got good eyes to have spotted him.'

'Come on, we'll go and see.  It's a mountaineer, I suppose—but no one ever scales those rocks.  They always climb from the other side of the valley.  It's odd ! '

They walked along the ridge and soon reached the foot of the spur. Peter already had an idea of who the stranger might be, and as they drew nearer he became certain.

' That light-coloured shirt and corduroy trousers and the woolly cap on the side of his head can only mean one person. Yes, that's who it is—Rudi himself.'

' Who's he ? '

' Rudi Saax, a guide from the valley—you haven't met him yet—he's a good sort, you'll soon find out. But I'm a bit worried to see him prowling about here ; I can't think what he's up to on that spur of rock.'

' If he's a climber, surely he's climbing—it's obvious ! '

' You don't understand. They climb from the other side, as I told you before—he's not scaling anything. You've only to look at him to see that there's something queer going on.'

Peter was perfectly right. The whole attitude of the man clinging to the rock-face about twenty metres above them was strained and unnatural. He stood absolutely still on an overhanging projection, his raised hands clasping the rock and his head pressed sideways against it. His body seemed utterly lifeless, as if struck by lightning.

' It's odd that he hasn't heard us coming,' muttered Peter. ' We've certainly been making enough noise.'

17

' Perhaps something's wrong with him ! ' said Larry.

' That's hardly likely, otherwise he wouldn't be able to stay in that position. Wait a minute ; sometimes the guides go off on their own, as part of their training —but they usually go in the Doldenhorn direction, or towards the Fisistocke. What can he be doing here ? That peak has nothing special to interest a guide.'

They waited patiently but nothing happened, the man remained absolutely still. Peter was completely mystified and finally stepped forward, unable to bear it any longer.

' Hi there, Rudi ! What's going on ? '

It was just as if an electric shock went through the man clinging to the rock-face above them. The two boys saw him make a sudden movement and relax his hand-holds, and for a terrible moment they thought that he was going to fall backwards.

' He almost had it ! ' muttered Peter. ' We startled him. I just don't understand what he's doing there.'

The boy had turned pale, for accidents happen so quickly, and twenty metres is a considerable height. But the guide recovered himself ; it was a near thing, for he had to change his position, and they saw him easing his right leg into a narrow fissure so as to keep his balance. He turned his head and called out :

' Who is it ? '

' It's Peter ! '

' Well, what do you want ? '

He sounded really angry and Peter was at a loss as
to how to reply.

' Nothing ! We were just passing . . .'

' What's that you're mumbling ? '

Peter raised his voice : ' I was only saying that we
were out for a walk and we saw you, so we came over.'

' Well, be off with you—I've had enough of you ! '

' But what's the matter, Rudi ?  We're not doing any
harm.  Do listen.'

' I told you to scram ! '

The guide was shouting at them now, with his head
thrown back.  The two boys looked at each other,
not knowing what to make of things ; there was

something odd going on, something quite out of keeping with their own intentions, lending an exaggerated importance to the whole affair.

' Be off, I tell you ! '

Before the terrified boys could see what he meant to do Rudi began snatching up stones and hurling them with all his might in their direction. One fell just at Peter's feet, and it wasn't a small one.

' He must be crazy ! '

Peter was furious now and eager to retaliate, looking round for stones in his turn, but Larry tugged at his arm.

' Come on, Peter, we'd better go ; it's no use arguing with him.'

' Did you ever see such a lunatic ? He's raving mad ! What on earth's got into him ? What have we done to upset him ? '

They were some way off now, with Peter still grumbling away, swearing furiously in a dialect that Larry could not understand. The contrast between Peter's slow sing-song manner of speech and the violence of what he certainly must be saying struck Larry as very funny, and he burst out laughing : ' Oh, Peter, you're priceless ! I wish you could see yourself ! Marvellous, what goes on in these mountains ! '

' There's nothing to laugh at. I've never seen Rudi act this way before. Something must be up—I'll tell Father about it tonight.'

Having come through a copse of stunted pines at the edge of the Golitschen meadows, they stopped and looked back. Rudi still stood in the same place, and from that distance he looked like a puppet stuck on to the rocks. He was as motionless as when the boys first set eyes on him, and they stayed looking at him for a long while, wondering what his strange behaviour meant and what he was planning to do.

'He can't mean to spend the night on that little platform of rock, he'll simply have to move!' Peter decided.

'We've only got to wait long enough—we'll soon see!'

They nearly lost patience, and dusk was already beginning to fall over the other side of the valley when Rudi finally made a move. They saw him crouch down on his platform and begin the descent, very, very slowly. His movements were jerky and uncertain and he seemed to be feeling his way carefully before taking hold. Occasionally he paused and flattened himself against the rock-face, as if he were afraid of the slight drop beneath.

'Larry, don't you think it looks as if he's got cold feet?'

'Why? It seems perfectly natural to me to go slowly, the rock-face is almost vertical.'

'Nonsense—it's easy to see that you don't know him. That little spur is nothing to a chap like Rudi Saax;

21

it's full of good solid holds and ordinarily he would come down in a couple of shakes—he climbs like a cat. That's why I can't understand what's happening.'

Meanwhile Rudi had at last reached the end of his climb, after a good many more pauses. He glanced up once more at the peak above him and started off down the Golitschengrat towards the path leading to the valley.

' Well, it's all very odd ! I wonder what Father will think when we tell him about it. He knows Rudi well and he'll find it hard to believe.'

The two friends started on their homeward journey. It was already getting late and the sun had gone down behind the First peak ; the cool shades of evening were stealing over the mountain and the fresh breeze rising from the valley made them shiver.

' We must get a move on now,' said Peter. ' If Father is back from haymaking he'll box our ears for not having brought in the cattle.'

Luckily the chalet was not far off. They caught sight of it a little below them, lying in the shelter of a ridge which protected it from northerly winds. Larry still had one question to ask, however.

' Listen, Peter, what did you mean just now ? You seemed fed up at seeing the guide climbing *your* Alp.'

' Oh, it would take too long to explain—Rudi's a good chap, but I know why he's always climbing in this direction, and I don't like it. He's tracking the chamois, the mountain goat, you know, the male of the herd that comes to graze every year around here. I was the first to discover them, two years ago. They hadn't been seen on this side of the valley for ages, so you can imagine how exciting it was when I found them again ! But Rudi is a sportsman as well as a guide and he stalks them all over the mountain, especially the he-goat. That's why I don't like seeing him on my Alp, although no one's seen the goats about yet this year.'

' But what can *you* do to stop him finding them ? '

' Oh, there are various ways. Rudi and the chamois have come to grips already, last year in the spring, but that's a long story—Father ought to tell you about it. He probably will in any case, once he hears what's happened this afternoon. That was strange enough in all conscience.'

' Do tell me about it ! '

' No. Father would be cross if I told you myself, and it's getting late. I know we've an excuse, but we mustn't push our luck. Here are the cattle now. You promised to round them up, so get going ! I'll run to the chalet to ring the bell, to help bring them in.'

' Mind you don't tell the whole story before I get back ! '

' Don't worry ! I'll wait till everyone's there ! '

Peter dashed off, while Larry, seizing a thick branch to use as a stick, started to drive the animals home.

*Rudi of the Mountains*

He delayed just a few moments to savour his solitude. Within an hour, night would fall ; the shadow was already deepening over the wooded slopes, while high up above, the snowy peaks glowed in the setting sun.

1,844
F
R

## 3

## *Larry Brings the Cattle Home*

When Peter reached the Golitschenhut, Mother Gruber
was busy pressing a huge block of fresh gruyère cheese
into its mould. Uli, Peter's eight-year-old younger
brother, and Rose-Marie, his baby sister, were watching
the proceedings intently, but broke off to welcome their
big brother with shouts of joy.

'Well, my son!' said his mother. 'You've certainly taken your time!'

She was a slim, energetic woman, always on the go,
for there is a great deal to do on a mountain pasture,
even for an excellent housekeeper, with all her wits
about her.

'It wasn't our fault, Mother! We had a queer kind
of adventure. I'll tell you all about it. Isn't Father
back yet?'

'No, he isn't, luckily for you—he'd very likely have
boxed your ears!'

She did not really mean this, however, for Father
Gruber was the kindest and calmest of men, and if
it had come to that she would certainly have sprung

25

IMMACULATA COLLEGE
HAMBURG, NEW YORK

to the defence of her big son, whom she adored. But the Gruber family were fond of teasing each other.

' What have you been up to now ? ' she went on. ' You look thoroughly excited. And where's Larry ? '

' I left him higher up, bringing in the cattle. It's quicker like that. We'll tell you the whole story when Father's here. I'll ring the bell now to call in the herd ! '

He sprinted up the ladder leading to the hayloft above the dairy where the cheese was made. About twenty cowbells stood there, lined up on the floor. Peter seized the largest of all, which belonged to the queen of the herd ; this was rung every evening outside the cattle-shed and when the cows heard it they began moving slowly of their own accord towards their shelter for the night. They had long grown used to this procedure, which saved the trouble of running about looking for them all over the pasture.

Peter was on the point of coming down again with the big bell under his arm when he heard terrific shrieks going on outside, which startled him so much that he nearly dropped everything. The shrieks turned into howls and cries for help, and for a moment everyone stood rooted to the spot—Peter on his ladder, his mother bending over the huge copper cooking pot and the two younger children clinging to their mother's skirts—then as the howls grew nearer, they rushed forward all at once, and this is what they saw.

Larry was hurtling down the mountain pasture as fast as he could, arms and legs flying, leaping over hillocks and rhododendron bushes as if the devil was at his heels. Behind him galloped one of the cows, with head lowered and horns at the ready, while Larry shrieked : ' The bull ! The bull ! '

It seemed a desperate situation, but Peter, who had jumped down the three stone steps to his friend's rescue without knowing what was happening, suddenly stopped short, completely transfixed, and then burst into peals of laughter that echoed over the mountain and drowned Larry's anguished cries for help. Behind him the other three began guffawing in their turn. Altogether they set up a splendid chorus, and the jackdaws nesting in the rocks up above must have flapped their wings in fright.

Peter was doubled up with laughter, but just managed to catch hold of Larry as he dashed by, wild with fright—otherwise he would have rushed full tilt into the house.

' Oh, Larry, you'll be the death of me ! ' gasped Peter, laughing so much that he could hardly speak.

Larry himself began to smell a rat when he saw them all shrieking with laughter, especially as the terrifying beast at his heels had come to a standstill some way away from the chalet. He felt rather annoyed that no one seemed to appreciate the danger he had just escaped.

Still out of breath, he managed to stammer : ' It's all very well for you to laugh—supposing the bull had . . .'

' The bull ! Oh no, I can't bear it ! ' Peter began laughing harder than ever.

' Stop it, Peter ! ' said his mother. ' Can't you see that Larry's badly upset ? You'd better tell him what it's all about.'

So they took Larry into the living-room. He was still puzzled and cross, but Peter managed to calm him down and finally persuaded him to share the joke.

' It wasn't the bull, Larry, only a cow—a perfectly harmless old cow who wouldn't have hurt you for the world ! '

' That's what *you* think. I'd like to have seen you coping with her ! All I did was poke her with a stick, then she turned on me and began to charge.'

' She wasn't charging, you idiot ! How could she—it was only Rose, a soppy old cow who always wants to be stroked when she sees someone coming.'

' How was I to know ? '

' Well, you only had to scratch her nose a bit and give her a friendly pat or two, then she'd have left you alone. The idea of taking poor old Rose for the bull ! If you could have seen yourself . . .'

' All you can do is laugh—ha, ha, ha—it's beastly of you.'

' Keep your hair on, Larry—can't you see how funny

it was ? Poor Rose would be awfully sorry if she knew what a fright she'd given you.'

' I wasn't frightened—don't make things up.'

' Don't make things up yourself—you've never run so fast in your life before ! '

Larry saw the funny side at last and decided to take the whole thing in his stride as just another of his Alpine holiday adventures.

' All right, it *was* a good joke, but I shan't get caught like that again ! Now I'll go and change my shoes.'

' Look out for the real bull, all the same ! '

With a final burst of laughter Peter took hold of the big bell, and went to get the cattle in.

Larry went up to his room. He was very fond of this weather-beaten hut, perched high in the Alps, and would not for the world have deserted it to spend his holidays in the Grubers' comfortable house at Kandersteg, which his parents had rented for a month. When he came to the Golitschenalp he had been prepared to find something very simple, for at 700 metres above sea level no one goes in for luxury or even for much comfort. Nevertheless he had not expected anything quite as bare and primitive as the rooms which Peter had proudly shown him on his arrival. There was no furniture except for a big table and two rough wooden benches. The few clothes they had with them hung from nails stuck at random into the wooden panels lining the thick stone walls. Two plank beds stood in

30

the parents' room, and in the children's room there were bunks with old straw mattresses. There was a makeshift look about it all, even an impression of poverty, although the Grubers were really quite comfortably off.

It just suited Larry. He had not come to the mountains to loll about on a featherbed, as he said ; all he wanted was to live the same simple life as the Alpine people themselves, miles away from the city and the myriad restrictions of civilisation. Up here he was free at last !

He sat down on the straw mattress which had been allotted to him in a ' ground-floor ' bunk near the narrow window overlooking the valley, and changed his shoes. He had almost forgotten his recent adventure. Certainly he hadn't come out of it well, but what did that matter ? He was still new to the mountains and it was only natural that he should make mistakes.

Just as he rejoined the others, Father Gruber himself appeared, carrying on his back a huge bale of hay tied up in a cloth knotted at the corners like a handkerchief. ' My word, it's hot ! Good evening, all ! ' Shaking off his bundle, he wiped the sweat from his face with his sleeve, and puffed : ' That's enough for today ! That lower slope almost killed me—I thought I'd never get to the end of it. Hi there, Peter, bring me a big cup of cold tea, and then we'll eat.'

Father Gruber had not shaved for two days, having

31

no time to waste on such frivolities, and the beginnings of a black beard darkened his weather-beaten sun-tanned face still more. He had very light blue eyes, whose gaze lingered on all they saw, very short hair sticking out in all directions and a breadth of shoulder that is typical of the mountains.

Larry was very fond of ' Uncle ' Fritz : he was slow to get started, but quick-witted, calm and collected, and always ready for a joke.

' What was all that yelling I heard just now ? You were making such a din they must have heard you over at Kandersteg ! '

Immediately everyone began telling the story of the bull, bursting out laughing all over again, and this time Larry joined in the joke against himself wholeheartedly and laughed as loud as anyone. Father Gruber finally put an end to the fun by taking his place at table and calling loudly for his evening meal.

Larry had never eaten with such appetite nor enjoyed his food so much as on the Golitschenalp, yet Mother Gruber's meals were not banquets : this evening there were potatoes cooked in the big smoky pot, known as *rösti* in those parts, a hunk of bacon standing on the table and cheese in its huge mould for everyone to cut at. The spoons and forks were thrust behind a leather band fastened to the wall, sharp knives were stuck into the wooden panels, and everyone helped himself. Larry loved it all.

No sooner had they sat down than Peter began describing their afternoon's adventures, somehow forgetting to say anything about the fissure through which they had made their descent. Father Gruber was immediately all ears. Rudi was a great friend of his and when they were both young they had explored the mountains together, so he was deeply interested in the story.

'What an extraordinary thing! It's not a bit like him. Yes, he's certainly changed since his adventures last spring, Heaven knows.'

Larry took up his cue here, remembering Peter's words to him on their return journey. 'What happened, Uncle Fritz?' he asked. 'Peter said something about stalking a chamois.'

'That's right! Didn't he tell you too that the chamois belonged to him?' Father Gruber answered, laughing. 'Peter looks on it as his very own. You see, Larry, it was he who found the chamois herd first, and he can't bear anyone else to go near them. Friend Rudi doesn't agree, and so they squabble about it every time they meet. I'm not surprised he didn't like your turning up.'

'It was more than that, Father! He was absolutely furious, wasn't he, Larry? I've never seen him in such a state before, and there was no sign of the chamois. Anyway Rudi won't find him, I'll take care of that.'

' Just listen to him ! Rudi is cleverer than you, my boy. And you're forgetting one thing : the chamois is even cleverer than Rudi and he doesn't need you to help him. You'll see what I mean, Larry, when you hear the story I'm going to tell you. Let's go out on to the verandah—it's still daylight and we'll be more comfortable there. I must have some air, these rooms are stifling.'

# 4

## Rudi and the Mountain Goat

They went out on to the covered verandah which runs along one side of all Bernese chalets. Young Uli had been to fetch his father's meerschaum pipe and tobacco pouch.

'Do you mind, Lise?' Father Gruber asked his wife. 'Just one more pipe and it'll be the last!'

Then he turned to Larry and said: 'Now I'll tell you the story of Rudi and the Almengrat chamois, and you will see how impossible it is to catch up with that animal.'

The others knew it all by heart, but nevertheless they gathered round Father Gruber as eagerly as if they were going to hear a completely new tale. He took his time filling his pipe, setting the scene like a good story-teller who is quite certain of his audience's whole attention.

They made a perfect family group, Larry thought, like the illustrations in old-fashioned annuals—the two younger children sitting at their father's feet, the mother smiling gently, and Peter leaning casually against the wall. Larry smiled too as Father Gruber's story got under way.

' Last year, spring came very early, and although we didn't quite trust our luck we came up to the mountain pasture a week sooner than usual, to make the most of the warm weather. An extra week isn't to be sneezed at, and we're always in a hurry to get here. We'd only just settled in—I think it was the second day after we arrived, if I remember rightly—when I climbed up towards the First mountain to see how the enclosures had fared during the winter; for you understand, Larry, sometimes one gets unpleasant surprises—rocks break away from the ridge when the thaw comes, taking part of the enclosure with them, stakes and fences crumble to pieces, wires rust away, goodness knows what else! But we were certainly lucky last year, there was very little damage done, and by midday I had finished patching things up, so I said to myself : " It might be an idea to cross over on to the Almen to say hullo to Harry—he comes from Frutigen —and get news of them all down there." For everyone stays by his own fireside all winter, and winter lasts a long time in these parts.'

' Perhaps you also hoped that Harry might give you a drink ! ' put in Mother Gruber.

' Perhaps I did, Lise, perhaps I did ! The old rascal always has something by him and it doesn't do to let people drink alone, it makes them sad.'

36

He went on with his tale, explaining that he had climbed up to the col where snow was still lying, especially on the other side at the foot of the Almengrat, where indeed the sun never penetrates the lower slopes until high summer. Even then patches of soft snow can be found in the shelter of a rock or in the depth of a crevice.

'To cut a long story short, I pressed on as far as the hut and found Harry. He had only just arrived, and was in the throes of getting settled. Everything was at sixes and sevens, just like home! There was no chance of our having a quiet drink together, so we just shook hands, and I picked up some of his news and said goodbye. He didn't know which way to turn. For my part I had plenty of time, it was a beautiful day and when I caught sight of the saffron piercing through the snow high on the mountain pasture I made up my mind to have a closer look, it was so pretty. I sat down on a rock at the foot of the col to have a bite of lunch, basking in the sun like a lizard, thinking what a grand life it was in the mountains, that it looked like being another fine summer . . . and so on. We're fond of day-dreaming up here, you know, even if we don't get much time for it.'

It was then that Father Gruber caught sight of the chamois, who had ventured unusually far down the mountain in search of fresh young grass, and was grazing hardly more than 300 metres away from

Harry's hut. The chamois was without any doubt the leader of the herd, which Peter had discovered the year before, and Father Gruber was able to take a good look at him. The animal was grazing peacefully, oblivious of all the activity going on round the hut.

Suddenly, however, Father Gruber saw the chamois's head jerk up, then the goat sprang into the air and bounded off towards the Almengrat slope. At the same moment a shot rang out, with a clear staccato sound that echoed all round the mountains.

' " That's Rudi having another shot at the chamois," I said to myself, "and he's missed again too ! " You see, Larry, the summer before, Rudi used to climb up here whenever he could spare the time from his work as a guide. It was the first time chamois had been seen on this side of the valley for I don't know how many years, and there's no one like Rudi for getting on their trail. The rest of us had scarcely caught a glimpse of the herd before Rudi turned up in the neighbourhood, and it was the male goat that he was after. He tracked him down all summer long, but without any luck. He could have caught up with some of the others but they just didn't interest him. That's why I wasn't surprised to hear his shot ; I knew that he couldn't be far away, and just then he appeared from behind the rocks at the top of the path leading up from the valley. He daren't come any further on to the mountain, because the male goat, who hadn't turned a hair at all Harry's commotion, would have picked up Rudi's scent immediately and would have disappeared like a streak of lightning. For he knew Rudi only too well—as you'll understand from the rest of the story.'

Father Gruber paused for a few minutes to relight his pipe : it was the right moment for a pause in any case, since the leading character had just appeared on the scene. It was growing colder too, and the whole group gathered more closely round the story-teller.

' Such an extraordinary thing happened then, Larry, that I'd never have believed it if someone else had told me the story. But it's perfectly true. I saw it happen with my own eyes.'

Rudi was on the other side of the Alp, too far away for Father Gruber to join him. Harry had come to the door of his hut when he heard the shot but hadn't seen the guide, so that Rudi set off alone on the chamois's track.

The male goat, who had been standing perfectly still on a patch of snow, had bounded swiftly to safety when he found himself within rifle shot, and had now come to a halt once more at the edge of the snow-covered rocks. When Rudi drew near, scrambling along the base of the ridge, and dropped on one knee to take aim, the chamois once more leapt out of range with a terrific bound, springing from slab to slab, from ledge to ledge, as far as the ridge itself.

' Then, my friends, I began to understand what was happening. At first when I saw the chamois halting so often I thought that he would be caught and I felt like calling out to him : " Look out ! Be off as fast as you can ! He'll get you ! " But when I saw him standing on the ridge, as still as a statue, I realised what he was up to. He, too, was playing a game. He knew that Rudi was his enemy and he was setting the pace, luring him into his own country—literally leading him on and forcing him to follow—in fact the hunted was setting a trap for the hunter, if you can believe it ! The gun no longer counted—all that mattered was who turned out to be the better climber, the chamois or Rudi. They were well matched, for Rudi is one of the best climbers in the countryside, and as much at home in the mountains as the chamois himself. I was too far away to intervene ; I could hardly make them out as they stood on the ridge, and I wondered how on earth it was all going to end.'

It might have ended badly for Rudi, for the rock-face was covered with *verglas* and the guide needed all his mountaineering craft and knowledge of climbing to stay the course—though Father Gruber only realised this afterwards. Another shot rang out, but the animal lured the hunter higher and higher, obviously plotting his downfall. Suddenly came the climax : Rudi had stepped on to a narrow downward-sloping ledge and was clinging to the rock-face just above the central couloir. The chamois had gone ahead and seemed to be waiting for him at the foot of the little gendarme rock which marked the end of the ridge. Perhaps Rudi lost his head, exhausted by this wild chase, and so made some mistake: Father Gruber saw him waver, fling his arms forward and tumble head first into space. Luckily for him, the couloir still had a thick blanket of snow, so that although he fell nearly ten metres the snow broke his fall. Like a dislocated puppet he slid faster and faster down the steep snow-covered slope leading to the mountain pasture.

' What happened next ? '

' Well, I was horrified, as you can imagine ! All sorts of weird ideas come into your head at such times. I think I must have cried out: " The chamois has beaten him! He's beaten him!" without fully realising that it was my friend Rudi who had just fallen, but at the same time I made for Harry's chalet as fast as I could, knowing that we must get up there to help Rudi.'

But Rudi's luck held. It took Father Gruber, Harry and his son nearly an hour to reach the heart of the mountain pasture, and as they drew near they saw the guide sitting in the snow nursing one of his legs. He caught sight of them on their way up and called out to them: ' It's nothing ! It's nothing ! '

' What a lucky escape Rudi had—to fall like that and

come out of it with nothing worse than a twisted ankle !
Of course, once he landed he simply slid on down
the snow-covered slope, but all the same . . . He was
rather ashamed of himself, poor chap, and it was the
dickens of a job getting him back to the chalet first of
all, and then down into the valley.'

But the strangest and most disturbing part of the
story was the discovery they made after reaching Rudi.
Harry noticed it first of all and pointed it out to Father
Gruber. There in the snow, round the spot where the
guide had lain for several moments in a dead faint,
were the marks of the chamois's hooves. There was no
doubt about it—the animal had come down from his
rocky perch to prowl round his victim.

' It's incredible ! I'd never have believed such a
thing. And I'm convinced that for an animal to behave
like that is quite extraordinary. There you are—that's
the whole story of Rudi and the chamois.'

' It's amazing,' said Larry. ' Rudi certainly was
lucky.'

' I'll say he was ! But it didn't teach him a thing,
for he has sworn to nail the chamois's head over the
door of his chalet. And he hasn't climbed once, pro-
fessionally, since the beginning of the season. All
he does is to roam about the mountain pastures,
stalking the chamois. But you needn't worry, Peter,
he won't catch him. No one has seen the herd yet
this year.'

' Of course he won't catch him ! ' muttered Peter. ' I mean to see that he doesn't, too. But he's furious at being outwitted.'

' I'm on your side, Peter, whatever happens,' put in Larry. ' There'll be two of us now to spike his guns ! '

' Well, meanwhile, you'd better go to bed,' decided Father Gruber. ' It's very late, and the sun will rise early tomorrow—come on, everyone, bedtime ! The story's finished and so is my pipe.'

They got up quickly, all the more readily because since nightfall it had become very cold, even though it was summer. Larry gave a last glance at the darkened scene : the star-spangled sky, the peaks of the ridge disappearing into the night, the lacy black silhouettes of the larch trees and the deep silence of the mountain brooding over all, eternally alone.

That night Larry dreamt of chamois and stalkers, and of climbing rocks overhanging fearful chasms. He could not guess, when he woke next morning, that these nightmares were not just reflections of past happenings but were also a warning : coming events cast their shadows before.

## 5

## *Tracking the Herd*

During the days that followed no one spoke of Rudi the guide and his adventure. The weather was set fair and there was a great deal to do. The animals had to be taken out early each morning. Father Gruber made hay on the steep slopes at the foot of the mountain pasture ; and there was the house to be kept clean. The wire fence round the enclosure had to be checked— Peter's work, in which Larry helped him—the soft cheese simmering in the enormous copper cauldron had to be stirred and the huge gruyère moulds in the dark-room had to be turned daily.

Thus every day brought its fresh task. Larry, who fitted in perfectly to the mountain life, took his full share of the work, yet the two boys still had time to go off on long expeditions, returning towards evening dog-tired, thirsty, sunburnt and drunk with air. Larry had never been so happy in his life.

They had not forgotten the chamois and during their rambles they scanned the slopes and fallen rocks hoping to catch sight of the herd—but in vain. Peter began to despair, thinking that the chamois must have stayed on the other side of the valley. Then, just when they least expected it, the thrill came !

One afternoon, while the family were lingering round the table after the midday meal, young Uli burst into the room in a great state of excitement, exclaiming :

' I've seen the goat ! I've seen the goat ! '

This woke them up with a vengeance, for they had been feeling rather drowsy after the long morning in the open. Without a word, Peter shot out of the house, and as he went, nimbly unhooked the field-glasses that always hung beside the door.

Father Gruber burst out laughing.

' Peter hasn't lost much time, I must say. He's got that animal on the brain, Larry ! '

' Do you think it can be Rudi's chamois ? '

' Of course it is ! He always blazes the trail.'

' I'll go and see.'

Larry went out on to the verandah and saw his friend ensconced behind the drinking-trough, field-glasses at the ready, scrutinising the medley of rocks, larch plantations and grassy patches at the foot of the Golitschengrat. Peter grumbled to himself, leaning his elbows on the edge of the trough, then suddenly he shouted :

' There he is ! I can see him. It's the chamois.'

Larry went up to him and said : ' Where is he ? Do let me see ! '

45

'Wait a minute. I must have another look. Yes, that's the chamois all right! Isn't he splendid?'

Peter was beside himself with excitement, and Larry could bear it no longer.

'Come on, give me the glasses!'

'No, you'd much better try to spot him without them, otherwise you won't see him. You have to be used to them. I'll tell you how to make him out. Do you see that little patch of snow like a triangle just under the ridge? Follow the base of the triangle towards the left and you'll come to a big rock—have you got it? Go on a bit further and you'll see two little larch trees. Just by the one on the left.

'I've got it. A tiny brown speck—it's moving!'

'Yes, that's the chamois! Now have a look through the glasses.'

Larry took hold of them in his turn and focussed them on to the rock-face. He saw the whole thing in perfect detail, as if it had suddenly come close to him. He moved the glasses slowly along, over the patch of snow, the big rock, the larches and finally shouted:

'There he is! I've got him!'

The chamois seemed to be right before his eyes, only a few yards away. Thanks to the glasses he could take the animal unawares and observe all his movements closely, and it gave him a tremendous thrill to watch a creature ordinarily so difficult to reach, without his knowing anything about it.

46

Peter was perfectly right : the chamois was splendid. He had a glossy fawn coat, glistening in the sunshine, curved black horns set well forward, a fine head and powerful shoulders. Larry was acutely aware of the speed and spirit expressed by the animal's whole appearance—his sure but delicate feet, his quivering awareness, his love of space and freedom. ' My very first chamois ! What a marvellous piece of luck ! ' said Larry to himself.

Meanwhile Peter was stamping with impatience.

' Hurry up ! We'll try and get nearer to him.'

' You're sure it is the one you're after ? '

' Of course I am. He's the finest of the lot ! Wait a minute, I'll just tell them we're going. Mind you don't lose sight of him ! '

It didn't take him a minute to rush over to the chalet, tell his parents, snatch up a rucksack, stuff a hunk of bread and two apples into it and dash back.

' Come on, Larry ! We'll get on his trail. He won't stay on the Golitschen, he must have left the herd on the Almen slopes, and he's sure to cross over by the little col at the foot of the First mountain. We'll go straight there, keeping our eyes on him all the time, it'll take us less than an hour. We may even get to the col before he does, if we don't startle him too soon. In any case, he'll take us to the herd. There must be two or three females and some of their young camouflaged among the Almengrat rocks. If we found them,

47

it would be terrific ! They often stay in the same place for several days, and we could go back there.'

The two friends walked along side by side fairly swiftly in a direction almost opposite to that in which the chamois was.

' Let's go the long way round,' decided Peter. ' We'll be less likely to startle him, and it isn't so steep. It's longer, but safer.'

The chamois was still high up above them, under the little larch tree. He progressed slowly, driven by greed, through the highest grassy patch of the mountain. The boys took care to keep him in sight as they walked along.

It had been tricky enough to make out the tiny brown speck in the jumble of rocks, with their changing light and shade, but once the chamois was found, it was simple to keep him in view ; their glance returned unfailingly to the same spot with surprising ease and speed.

' It was clever of Uli to spot him—he must have very good eyesight.'

' He certainly has ! It can't have been easy and we might have missed him.'

The two friends had already gone quite a long way and the path was gradually growing steeper. They hardly spoke any more, for Peter set quite a good pace. Their chalet had dropped out of sight some moments ago, hidden by rising ground.

48

They were alone on the mountain now, alone at the foot of the steep rocky walls which rose before them like huge stone cathedrals.

Larry realised perfectly that the whole vast landscape was far more than man-size, yet at the same time he was intoxicated with the mad mountaineering enthusiasm which comes to men alone on great heights. He was infatuated with the mountains; in a fortnight they had converted him from a tame town-dweller to a dare-devil who was game for anything.

They had reached the foot of the Golitschengrat's northern ridge, and now they had simply to follow its course as far as the col. They were just about to set foot on the rough path across the rock when Peter suddenly stopped dead.

' Look, Larry! He's on the move—it looks as if he's going away.'

The pale faraway speck was certainly moving fast. Peter raised his field-glasses, which he had taken care to bring with him.

' Yes, he's going further up. No—he's stopping— it looks as if something's startled him—he's obviously on the alert. Now he's moving by leaps and bounds towards the col.'

Larry could follow all the chamois's movements with his naked eye. He saw him spring up the slope, pause uncertainly, his head turned towards the pasture, and then set off towards the col. Again as they watched

49

he stopped for a moment, framed in the hollow of a rock, before disappearing over the other side of the ridge, as if sucked down into space.

The two boys looked at each other speechlessly. Then Larry shrugged his shoulders, saying : ' Well, that's that. We'll be too late. He's got away.'

Peter was furious. It was too stupid to have lost him just as they had found him !

' Wait a minute, there's still something we can do— but it's no good climbing up to the col, it would take too long. We should have to climb down the other side too, for you can't see much from up there, and we're hardly likely to find the herd calmly waiting for us. We'd have no chance of taking them by surprise.'

' What on earth shall we do then ? '

' Do you remember the fissure we came down the other day ? We might try and climb up that way ; it would bring us out on to the ridge, and I bet we'd discover the whole herd without their seeing us. You're not afraid, are you ? '

' Afraid ? Of course not ! ' protested Larry indignantly.

' All right then, let's go ! We shall get a marvellous view from up there—don't you think it's a good idea ? '

' I certainly do ! ' Larry declared. ' It's a super idea ! What are we waiting for ? '

Peter hooted with laughter.

' Get along with you ! Just because you've done a

bit of rock climbing you needn't think you're a mountaineer! But don't worry—I'll keep an eye on you and it isn't any more difficult to climb up the fissure than to climb down it. Don't let's waste any more time. Follow me and let's get a move on.'

They began rushing down the slope, faster and faster, each bound serving as a springboard to the next. Larry rolled over and over in the lush grass but Peter did not even look round, for once launched on such a wild gallop it is difficult to stop. The ground began rising again near the stream, however, and they gradually slowed down.

' What a mad rush ! ' panted Larry. ' I almost broke my neck ! '

' Nonsense ! ' exclaimed Peter. ' There's nothing to it. The whole secret is to let yourself go. Have an apple. If you like, we could rest a little.'

' No, thanks, I'm thirsty but not a bit tired. What do you take me for ? I don't want to rest ! '

' All right, let's press on then. The sooner we reach the ridge the better. We're not far off.'

In a couple of strides they crossed the stream cascading between the stones and reached the rockface.

' Now we'll *really* see what you can do,' said Peter.

# 6

## *The Razor-blade*

They came to a halt at the foot of the fissure and Larry glanced up at it apprehensively.

It wasn't very high, at least it didn't seem to be, nor was it completely sheer but definitely sloped to join the ridge; nevertheless, the climb wasn't something to be undertaken lightly.

' Well, Larry, what's the verdict ? Can you manage it ? It's not dangerous, I promise you, and you saw for yourself when we climbed down the other day that there are plenty of holds.'

' I'm not afraid—what an idea ! Come on, lead the way ! '

' No, I'll bring up the rear, then I can watch out for you.'

' All right, then, let's go.'

So Larry went ahead into the fissure. He wasn't nervous, only excited, for it was just the kind of adventure he had always dreamt of. His first climb !

He pressed himself into the rocky opening, searching for a notch to cling to with his left hand and feeling for a hold with his right, then hoisted himself up, while his right foot instinctively fitted itself into a crack which seemed made for it.

' He's well away,' thought Peter.

Larry seemed to know by instinct just what to do, moving methodically and unhurriedly, never trusting to a fresh hold without first making sure of his three key supports. He went up and up, little by little, completely absorbed in what he was doing and not bothering about Peter, although he knew him to be just beneath. Concentrating on his movements and on his balance and the safety of his holds, he climbed with relative ease. Moreover, there were no real difficulties to overcome. But when they finally emerged on to the ridge at the end of ten minutes or so, one after the other, Larry was almost trembling with excitement.

' Did you see me, Peter ? It was terrific ! '

His cheeks glowed and his eyes shone with the thrill of his first climb, with his pride and joy at having conquered his fear, and with something of the true mountaineer's obsessive passion.

' You did splendidly ! ' said Peter warmly. ' Let's climb up a little further to the right—we'll be able to see better from there.'

At their feet lay the Almenalp, surrounded on all sides by high rocky peaks. They could see two little chalets far down below and could hear a faint tinkling of bells.

' Let's stop here a moment. There's a marvellous view, and we've simply got to find the brute.'

Peter fished the field-glasses out of the ruck-sack, which he'd slung round him when he started to climb. It took him a long time to make out the chamois and they almost gave up ; but after a painstaking search Peter finally caught sight of him through the glasses. He had moved far away from the col, right to the edge of the grassland, and had taken cover among the rhododendrons and dwarf arrolla pines which marked the transition from grassland to rocks ; this was why he had been so difficult to find.

Larry for his part could not see him with the naked eye because of the distance, and he was growing impatient about this when Peter exclaimed :

' He's joined the rest of the herd. I can see some of them a bit lower down. They're very well camou-flaged.'

' I can't see a thing.'

' Have a squint through the glasses. You'll soon find them.'

It really did look as if the whole herd were there. Larry could see several pale specks scattered among the bushes.

' But where is our chamois ? '

' Move the glasses to the right, towards the col. He's standing a little apart from the others—can you see him ? '

54

' Yes, now I can. But they're so far away that even with the glasses . . .'

' I'll tell you what we'll do—let's try to get up to them via the ridge. If we go down again they'll notice us and that'll be the end of that, but if we take the high road we stand a good chance. But we mustn't lose any more time, for the mist is beginning to rise.'

Since the beginning of the afternoon, in fact, the sun had turned a dead white, and scattered veils of mist were floating round the base of the mountain, threatening to cover the whole. The wind had risen some time ago and a great dark cloud was moving across the sky from distant Valais.

The two friends set off towards the col. At first all went well ; the going was not steep and the ridge was broad enough to be perfectly safe. Very soon they reached the first gendarme, a kind of turret-shaped peak completely blocking their path. They had to go round its base, by a winding path which luckily formed a ledge : but when Larry found himself alone on it, after Peter had made the trip, he came out in a cold sweat : it was so terribly narrow and on his right there was a steep drop down to the Golitschenalp.

' I mustn't think about it,' he said to himself. ' I just mustn't let myself think about it ! I must go on— if I stop I've had it ! I know I can do it—it's easy really—just one foot, then the other . . .'

It only took a minute to reach the other side of the

55

peak, though it seemed like an hour to him. He panted and puffed, and realised that he'd been holding his breath all the time.

' Gosh, that was something ! '

' What ? That was nothing ! Just don't think about the drop, Larry. The ledge was quite wide— almost a balcony, in fact ! Come on, let's get going again.'

' You're a nice one ! '

But Peter wasn't even listening. He had already started off, full of excitement at the thought of catching up with the chamois, and Larry had no choice but to follow him.

They reached a second gendarme, not so peaked this time and easier to circle, for it did not block the way completely.

' You see, it's child play ! ' declared Peter.

' If you say so—but I think your ridge is pretty tricky ! '

' Don't make such a song and dance about it. It's not kids' stuff, obviously, but there's nothing dangerous about it. Father wouldn't say a thing if he knew we were here.'

' Better not think about what he'd say, in my opinion ! '

They both laughed, but Larry was right : the ridge grew narrower all the time, and they soon found themselves moving along a sloping piece of rock no more than a metre wide, which finally brought them up short.

' A razor-blade ! ' grumbled Peter.

The spur of the ridge really did look like a razor-blade.

' Now we've had it,' cried Larry. ' We'll just have to go back. We ought to have gone by way of the pasture—it would have been better.'

' Yes, only to have scared the whole herd away before we got anywhere near them ! It wouldn't have been any use at all. But from up here . . .'

' Where's this got us to now, for Heaven's sake ? We shan't reach them one way or the other. We've missed out all along the line.'

' That's what you think, is it ? Well, you're wrong ! I'm not going to miss such a chance of taking them by surprise, and I specially want to know exactly what the herd consists of this year. We're pressing on ! '

' What ? ' Larry could hardly speak. ' You don't mean you're going to risk crossing this ? It's hardly wide enough for a foothold . . .'

' Oh, shut up ! There's only three metres or so and then it'll get wide, you'll see. It'll be like a high road all the way to the col. Of course we're not going to walk along it—Rudi taught me how to cross snags like this.'

' No, it's the limit ! We'll break our necks ten times over ! '

' Nonsense ! It's not so very difficult. You'll see.'

' There's a drop of fifty metres at least ! '

' What's that got to do with it ? We're not talking about the drop. It's exactly the same whether there's a drop of two metres or fifty. Watch me carefully now.'

And before the horrified Larry could protest, Peter was off. He grasped the rock with both hands, his fingers crooked over the top, and swung himself lightly backwards into space, planting the soles of his feet firmly against the rock-face. He flexed his arms several times, as if to test his pose, and began to laugh.

' You see how easy it is ! Just like sitting in an armchair. Now I'm going to travel sideways like a crab.'

To his horror, Larry saw Peter swinging gaily along, his feet well pressed against the rock, his body arched and his strong hands holding fast.

' Stop ! You terrify me ! '

' I'm only showing you how easy it is. Look out now—I'm putting on speed ! '

With swift movements of hands and feet Peter covered the length of the razor-blade in a few seconds. Larry began to think that it couldn't really be so bad after all, but when his friend called out to him from the further side ' Now it's your turn ! ', he protested ' You don't really think that I . . .'

' Don't worry ! ' Peter broke in. ' You saw how I

58

managed. The whole secret is to get a good grasp with
your hands, pulling yourself up as you go, and it's
just like being fastened to the rock. There's nothing
to be afraid of. Press the soles of your feet against the
rock, trust in your shoes—you won't slip, I promise
you! Come on now, get going! It'll only take you
ten seconds.'

Larry needed a good deal of persuading, however,
before he would risk it, and when he finally started it
was like jumping off at the deep end: he wasn't quite
sure what was happening, and he hardly heard Peter's
encouraging remarks, but moved as if in a daze,
without thinking of what he was doing. Then he felt
a firm hand seizing him by the collar, and there he was

on the other side of the razor-blade, out of breath and pale as death, with legs turned to jelly and a longing to burst into tears.

' That's fine, Larry ! You've made it ! You were great ! '

Larry gradually pulled himself together.

' Are you all right ? '

' Yes, much better now, thanks. But, Peter, I was in an awful funk ! '

Peter began to laugh and gave him a thump on the shoulders.

' Don't give it a thought ! You'll do. I won't deny that we were taking a bit of a risk. We really should have been roped—better not play that sort of game too often. But it was only three metres or so, after all, and the main thing is that we did it ! It's plain sailing now—we can get on.'

It wasn't exactly a high road, as Peter had claimed, but in comparison with the traverse they had just made it was easy going. Larry had recovered from his emotions and followed his friend calmly, for the ridge now stretched straight ahead towards the col without any stumbling-blocks.

Peter stopped suddenly by a pillar-like rock which abutted on to the Almenalp and said, pointing :

' Look, there they are—just below us—we don't need the glasses any more ! And they haven't noticed us—what luck ! We can get a good look at them now ! '

# 7

## The Goats in Danger

The two stalkers hid behind a little rock jutting out from the ridge and dug themselves in as comfortably as they could. The observation post they had chosen seemed ideal.

The herd, about a dozen strong, was assembled at the foot of the long slope leading from the First mountain, amidst some rhododendron bushes. The animals were wonderfully well camouflaged; indeed it had needed the young mountaineer's practised eye to make them out.

'Only three hundred metres away, Larry. Just think! I've never seen them so close! It's terrific!'

'It looks as if our chamois isn't there any more.'

'Oh, he must be somewhere about. They're always moving around, you know.'

It took them a moment or two to locate *their* chamois, however; he had gone a little apart from the herd and was standing perfectly still under a young larch tree, his head upright, calm and relaxed. He quivered now and then and his hocks trembled, and it was easy to see that even in repose he was constantly on the alert.

Larry watched him carefully through the glasses.

' Do you think they'll stay here long ? "

Peter didn't answer at once : he was scanning the surroundings. ' If we've been able to locate the herd,' he was thinking, ' very likely Rudi isn't far off.'

' We'd better see whether he's somewhere nearby ! ' he said. ' He has a flair for finding the chamois.'

' Who do you mean ? Rudi ? '

' Of course. He's probably prowling about over there.'

Suddenly he nudged Larry and whispered : ' What did I tell you ? There he is ! '

' Oho ! Are you sure ? '

' Of course I am ! Over there, to the right of that clump of trees—in the middle of the stream—can you see him ? '

' Yes, there's something moving.'

' It's Rudi ! Give me the glasses. He's climbing up by way of the stream—he's being very careful— moving from rock to rock—and he's so cunning that he certainly won't dislodge a single stone. He must have located the herd from the opposite ridge, and then retraced his steps to the bottom of the pasture.'

' Has he got a gun ? '

' Yes, slung over his shoulder. But he's still too far away, he can't shoot from there.'

62

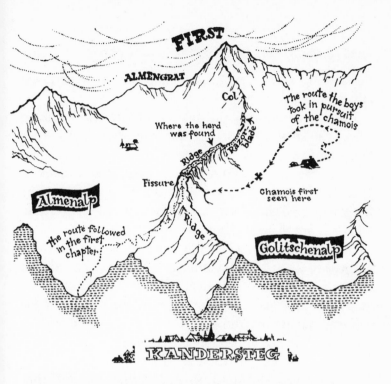

' And the chamois will realise he's there any moment now ! He won't even have time to unsling his gun.'

' The best part of it is that he doesn't know we're here. We'll only come out into the open after the animals have gone. I want him to know that we've been watching the whole thing—he won't like having eye-witnesses ! '

Perched in their hideout the two friends had a marvellous view and could see everything : the guide drawing nearer and nearer on their left and the animals just up above, quite unconscious of the danger

63

threatening them. None of them moved or betrayed any sign of alarm.

Rudi came steadily on, taking infinite care, making use of the smallest rock, not worrying about getting his feet wet, and gradually approached the herd.

' Any minute now and they'll scatter like a flock of jackdaws,' muttered Larry. ' I'll bet the leader of the herd will give the alarm first. He's in a key position, what's more, just in the angle of the stream.'

But in spite of what the boys expected, nothing seemed to disturb the chamois. The guide had almost reached the nearest animals : they saw him come to a stop behind a huge boulder right in the middle of the stream, unsling his gun and raise it slowly to shoulder-level, supporting himself against the rock.

Peter began to get worried.

' Whatever's got into them ? Why haven't they noticed him ? '

Perhaps he was still too far off and daren't come any nearer, they thought.

' But he's near enough, he's such a good shot. What can be the matter ? Of course, I've got it ! The wind is blowing off the First, worse luck, now that we're in for bad weather, and the chamois can't scent him.'

' I think it's all up, Peter, Rudi will win. Look, he's taking aim.'

' No, I can't bear it ! '

Peter suddenly stood up and gave a wild shout which

resounded over the Almengrat slopes. It had the same effect as a clap of thunder on a calm sky : the echo rolled from one ridge to the next, while the terrified animals sprang away in all directions with amazing speed, disappearing like a flash of lightning. One solitary shot rang out, but did not have a chance. The rhododendron plantation was deserted and the two boys could only see a few pale fawn specks dancing about among the fallen rocks on the other side of the pasture.

The leader of the herd had escaped !

Peter stood on his perch with his hands on his hips, roaring with laughter. Rudi for his part was beside himself with fury. Peter's shout had taken him by surprise, just as he held the chamois in his line of sight. His reaction had not been swift enough and before he had recovered from his surprise the leader of the herd had vanished.

The guide left his hiding-place and crossed the stream. He now knew who was responsible for his failure and swore at them ferociously, throwing back his head and brandishing his gun with both hands, the wind bearing his insults down towards the valley. Peter only laughed louder than ever.

But Larry, although he was delighted at the turn of events, felt a bit apprehensive : Rudi really looked threatening and was certainly not going to stop at insults. The time had come to make a getaway.

' Come on, Peter, he's going to let fly. We'd better make ourselves scarce ! '

' Nonsense ! ' guffawed Peter. ' What can he do to us ? I've a perfect right to yodel if I want to. It's not my fault if he was just going to shoot. The mountain's free for all, isn't it ? '

' Yes, yes, of course ! But if we go on plaguing him he'll really get angry and we'll only have ourselves to thank.'

' Get really angry ? Don't you think he's angry enough already ? It's certainly time we were thinking of making tracks—but don't get the idea that it's because of Rudi, or that I'm afraid of him, for goodness' sake ! Just look at the sky and the way the wind's blowing. It's going to rain soon and I don't think we'll make it home in time.'

They took a last look at the mountain. There was no longer any sign of life, except for Harry's cows far down below returning to their shed, and some jackdaws flying round the Bonderspitze's sharp peak.

Although Rudi's anger had been so violent, he seemed to have calmed down very quickly. He was sitting on the grass beside the stream, his head in his hands, perfectly still, as if nothing had happened.

' What's the matter with him ? ' Larry asked. ' It's not natural ! He ought to be chasing us.'

' He couldn't, we're too high up. He's probably wondering how to get his revenge and how to plan his next campaign. But the main thing is that our chamois is safe ! There's no point in waiting about any longer —otherwise we'll get it in the neck when we reach the chalet. We'll go by way of the col and climb down on the other side. It won't take us long and we'd better hurry up because of the rain.'

The ridge stretched ahead of them, straight and fairly wide, as far as the col. Larry was relieved, for he no longer felt in the mood for climbs as difficult as that which Peter had forced him into before they reached their goal. He'd been through quite enough for one day !

The next stage was child's play and they soon reached the foot of the huge rocky pillar which cut the ridge in half. On either side, the peaks sloped gently towards the two mountain pastures. They were at the col. Without a break they rushed madly down the Golitschenalp's long slope, to the accompaniment of Peter's triumphant yodels, reaching the chalet just as the rain began to fall.

They felt like conquering heroes and were so pleased with themselves that they looked forward confidently to a tremendous welcome—but they were making a big mistake.

## 8

## *Rudi Explains*

A fine rain fell steadily, pattering on the chalet roof.
The peaks seemed to have vanished, blotted out by
the thick curtain hanging over the mountain. From
far away, in the Valais direction, there came the rumble
of thunder. It had suddenly grown very cold.

When the boys entered the chalet they found the
whole company in the living-room, gathered round
the little iron stove, where Father Gruber had lit a
fire of sticks and bark. The two boys shook themselves
like wet puppies, for they hadn't managed to escape
the first heavy drops of rain. Peter couldn't wait to
describe their adventure.

'Father, we've had such a time! I wish you could
have seen the chamois.'

'I'm not interested in the chamois. I've seen quite
enough already.'

Father Gruber spoke slowly and heavily, pronouncing
his words carefully, and his tone was like a douche of
cold water.

'But . . .'

' But me no buts ! Will you kindly explain what you were doing up on the ridge ? '

' But . . . Father . . . we were stalking the chamois . . . and we . . .'

' The chamois was strolling about on the ridge ? Fancy ! Haven't I told you always to climb by the col—and only by the col ! '

' Yes, but we'd have been too late ! He'd already reached the other side ! We'd never have found him ! '

' So you took it into your head to climb up on to the ridge as if you were an expert, I suppose ! And not content with that, you both had to play at acrobats on the razor-blade ! Are you out of your mind ? We saw you from here and it was a fine sight, I can tell you. Your mother has been in a terrible state ! '

Father Gruber was extremely angry, without a doubt, thundering away at them and with each outburst thumping the table so hard that it shook. Peter stood glued to the spot and Larry wished the floor would open and swallow him up.

' But, Father, there was no danger ! Rudi showed me . . .'

' Oh, so that's what you thought ? My goodness, you seem to think you're the chief guide himself. No danger ! Don't give me that. I've crossed that razor-blade myself with Georg in my time and it hasn't changed, and we were roped together ! And now you've the cheek to tell me that there's nothing to it—

just a pleasant walk, I suppose, to stretch your legs ? Don't you realise what you were doing ? That's how accidents happen. You ought to know better than to get up to such tricks. You're more foolish than a boy from the city who's never seen a mountain. Just because Rudi has taken you along with him once or twice you needn't think you know everything ! You'll end by breaking your neck. I'm warning you for the last time—next time I'll give you a thrashing, you too, Larry, so that you won't be able to sit down for a week, and you'll never want to go in for acrobatics like that again. Do you understand ? '

' Yes, Father.'

Peter looked truly sorry and repentant and hung his head, but something in his father's tone, he hardly knew what, made him risk a peep. Father Gruber was still storming away but there was a twinkle in his eyes which didn't escape the boys, and Larry was almost sure that he saw him wink. What a relief ! Things weren't so bad after all.

In fact, although Father Gruber was cross, he wasn't quite as angry as he pretended to be. The scolding and table-thumping were principally for Mother Gruber's benefit, to set her mind at rest, for to tell the truth he was pleased to find the boys ready to take risks. ' It forms the character,' he liked to say.

Nevertheless, when Mother Lise had gone to get the supper ready, he added :

70

'The razor-blade isn't as sinister as all that, I grant you. Georg and I were roped because we were going on by the high ledge—but don't take too many risks all the same. There are less dangerous spots to play about in. You ought to learn how to calculate risks, Peter, and that one was a bit much—O.K. ? '

'Yes, but, Father, we only did it because of the chamois, otherwise we'd never have gone that way.'

'Just think things out more carefully next time. And now, tell us your story ! '

Peter needed no pressing and described their afternoon's adventure at great length, though without going into all the details of their climbing exploits. The climax of his story was his conviction that ' now the chamois has escaped for good ! '

' I don't know so much about that,' put in Father Gruber. ' It seems to me that Rudi was too far away. Otherwise the animals would have scented him.'

' No, Father, you're wrong there. The wind was blowing strongly off the mountain, in Rudi's favour. He was in a good position, perhaps just about as far away as possible, but you know what a crack shot he is. No, the game would have been up but for us ! '

' In that case, my boy, I rather think you'll have Rudi to reckon with. He won't let you off easily, you know, for the chamois means a lot to him.'

' O.K., let him come ! I'm ready for him—I can do as I please in the mountains. There's no law against

71

singing, so why shouldn't I shout ?   I've a perfect
right to, haven't I ?   No one stops him shouting on his
side.   If he missed, it wasn't my fault.'

' Hmm.   I don't think that's quite true.   In any case
you'd better look out for yourself these next few days,
otherwise the sparks will fly ! '

Just at that moment little Uli, who had been playing
on his own by the low fire in the cheese dairy, burst
into the room :

' Someone's coming !   It's Rudi ! '

' Help ! ' cried Father Gruber, rubbing his hands
together.   ' Now the fat's in the fire—we're going to
see some action ! '

In spite of his bravado, Peter was really rather
nervous, while Larry didn't quite know what attitude
to take.   There was bound to be a show-down and
what would be the outcome ?

Then they heard the clattering of heavy iron-shod
boots on the doorstep, and Rudi appeared on the
threshold.   He was soaking wet.

His short jacket had lost all its colour : his breeches
clung to his thighs and water was trickling down on to
his shoulders from the shapeless old felt hat which
he had exchanged for his usual woollen cap.   He had
left his gun at the door of the barn.

His face had a shuttered sullen expression and he
was frowning heavily as he muttered : ' Good evening ! '

Father Gruber was determinedly friendly.

' Good evening, Rudi! Come right in, come up to the fire. You look as if you need to dry out.'

' I'm all right, Fritz, thank you. I thought I'd better shelter here for a bit until the rain stops.'

' Of course! You can't possibly go on down in weather like this. Lise, will you get my woollen jerkin so that he . . .'

' It's not worth it, Fritz! I shan't be staying long.'

' Now look here—you can't go yet, get that into your head, so you're going to put on the jerkin and we'll dry your jacket for you. Lise, make a good hot pot of tea and don't forget the schnapps! We're going to warm you up inside and out.'

Rudi had not looked at the two boys since he came in. He drew one of the stools up to the stove, and it was only after putting on Father Gruber's jerkin and drinking a big bowl of boiling hot tea that he finally spoke to Peter.

' Well, Peter, that's that! I had the chamois in the sights of my gun, and but for you . . .'

He spoke in a sad, dead voice, as if he were thoroughly tired and miserable, and made no reproaches. Larry was filled with pity for him, without exactly knowing why. Rudi's whole aspect as he sat there resignedly, almost in despair, was that of a beaten man. Father Gruber was aware of this too, and he couldn't understand it, for, after all, it was only a question of a shot gone astray.

' Cheer up ! ' he said. ' Don't look so miserable, Rudi ! Obviously this rascal here deserves to have his ears boxed, but there are plenty more chamois for you to aim at—just take care that these wretched boys don't get in your way next time ! '

' It's not that, Fritz, old chap. I may as well tell you now that I'm convinced I'll never get him : it's beyond me. I'm finished.'

' What's that ? You must be out of your mind, Rudi ! I never heard anything so ridiculous ! '

Mother Gruber put in a word. ' Don't make too much of this, Rudi, please. I know Peter behaved very badly, but you have shot plenty of chamois already and you'll shoot them again.'

' No, no, Lise ! It's all over ! I don't care about the rest of the herd, but I wanted to get that chamois more than anything. There was something between us. I'd better tell you the whole story, for you're bound to hear it sooner or later—some people suspect it already.'

The guide's story was such a mixture of fact and fantasy that it was hard to tell what had really happened and what was due to his imagination.

' I've always said that the reason I fell last year while I was stalking that cursed chamois on the Almengrat was that I lost my footing on a ledge covered with verglas, but of course that's not true. As if I would fall because of verglas ! Why do you think I don't act as a guide any more, when it's my trade, and I love climbing ?  I was never happier than high up on a snow cornice with a client on the end of my rope—but now it's all over, Fritz, it's all over for good.'

' What on earth are you talking about ?  Why can't you climb as a guide any more ?  It's absolute nonsense.'

' Nevertheless, it's true.  It isn't that I don't *want* to climb any more, but that I *can't*.  You see, Fritz, I didn't fall because of verglas but because I was afraid. Do you understand ?  I, Rudi Saax, was so frightened that I let go, just like a child.  Imagine what would happen if I did that with a client at the end of my rope ! It doesn't bear thinking of.  Well, now you know the truth, and it's a great relief to have told you.'

Mother Gruber was the first to answer him.

' I don't believe you, Rudi ; no one could have kept his footing up there on that ice.'

' *I* could have, Lise !  I have crossed by the Blüm-lisalp slabs when they were covered with the worst verglas you can imagine, and it didn't worry me any more than ordinary frozen snow.  No, I know what I'm talking about : it was fear.'

' All right, that's what you say,' put in Father Gruber.  ' But why shouldn't it have been because you lost your balance, because you felt giddy, or were tired, or goodness knows what else ?  You had been stalking the animal all day long, so it wouldn't be surprising ! '

' No, I tell you ! '

' You're as obstinate as a whole herd of chamois,' grumbled Fritz.

' No, no, no ! Why won't you believe me ? The mountain began to spin round me and I let go ! '

There was a dead silence. Rudi had not turned his head and seemed quite oblivious of his listeners, as if he were talking to himself, reliving the scene on the Almengrat. It was almost night ; flickering firelight came from the mouth of the stove and only the floor was lit up in the dark room. Father Gruber stirred impatiently on the bench, far from satisfied with Rudi's version.

' You're imagining all this, you know. You ought to give things time to settle down, then you'll be able to start acting as a guide again before long, I'm sure. Just get back into training on your own first of all— you'll soon be telling me everything's all right.'

' Get back into training—that's what I've been trying to do, without saying a word to anyone. Climbing the Zackengrat ridge just like a beginner, and the Fisi chimneys ; that's what I was doing the other day, too, when the boys saw me. I simply couldn't go on then, and I felt so ashamed with them watching me. No, Fritz, I wish I could make you understand. Every time I take hold of the rock, I seem to see those two eyes staring at me, forbidding me to climb. I can't escape that cursed chamois—shooting him is the only way I can get rid of him.'

77

Nobody knew what to say : they were all at a loss, the story was so strange. Father Gruber muttered to himself and then broke the silence by calling out : ' Lise, bring the lamp—it's pitch dark ! '

' Yes, it's high time I went down to the valley—my jacket must be dry by now,' said Rudi.

' What an idea ! ' protested Mother Gruber. ' You'll spend the night here with us, we've plenty of room. I wouldn't dream of letting you go out again in this weather.'

' It's very kind of you, Lise, but . . .'

' Don't be so silly. It won't be the first time you've spent the night on the mountain. No one's expecting you down there.'

After a few more objections, Rudi let himself be persuaded to stay. The simple evening meal—thick potato soup, cheese and a big bowl of milk—was soon eaten. Nobody said another word about the chamois, and everyone went early to bed.

Rudi lay down on Peter's straw mattress, Peter having doubled up with little Uli, and Larry heard him tossing and turning for a long time. Larry himself found it difficult to sleep : he could hear the rain beating down outside relentlessly, and he seemed to see two glittering eyes staring at him out of the darkness, while before him stretched a steep ridge, narrow and untrodden.

# 9

## *Off to the Schneehorn Hut*

Mountain weather often changes overnight. The two friends got up early the next morning, after Father Gruber had taken the cattle out to grass and Rudi had set off for the valley; the boys could hardly believe their luck, for it was a glorious day.

The early morning sky was wonderfully clear and bright and the rocks shone as if not only washed but polished by the rain. The whole mountain pasture seemed aglow with fresh colours, and the sound of tinkling cowbells, echoing from far and wide, harmonised perfectly with the peace and beauty of the summer day. The two boys were struck dumb with the loveliness of it all, for opposite them soared the Blümlisalp, clothed in fresh snow, icily pure, serenely beautiful.

' It's magnificent, Peter! I never dreamt of anything so wonderful! '

But Peter did not respond: he was staring at the surrounding peaks and seemed miles away from the Golitschenalp.

' What's the matter ? asked Larry. ' You look so odd ! '

Peter shook himself and burst out laughing.

' It's nothing ! I was only day-dreaming . . . I can hardly bear it when I look at the mountain over there and realise how long I'll have to wait. You see, Larry, in four or five years I want to register as a porter for long expeditions ; Father's in favour of this and Rudi was going to take me on, but there's no knowing what'll happen, the way he is now. In any case, I'll train as a guide—I'm determined to be a guide, Larry ! Farming doesn't appeal to me one bit. But I've got to wait so long . . .'

' You're going to be a guide ! That's marvellous ! Will you take me on as a client ? '

' A clumsy beginner like you—not likely ! '

Peter aimed a playful blow at his friend, saying : ' Come on ! There's time enough to think of that. I've just had a splendid idea about something else ; I'll tell Father and I think he'll agree.'

' You and your ideas—I only hope this one isn't as crazy as the razor-blade adventure ! '

' Goodness, no, nothing like that ! ' Peter assured Larry, laughing.

' It's no use stalking the chamois now, after all the hullabaloo we made on the Almenalp yesterday. They certainly won't still be there patiently waiting for us ; they'll have moved away and we'd never

find them. They may come back again in a few days—
we'll just have to see. Meanwhile, I thought we might
go and visit my godfather, who's keeper of the Schneehorn Hut. What do you say ? '

' Super ! Do you think your father will agree ? '

' We'll soon find out.'

When the question was put to him, Father Gruber
demurred a little at first, just for appearance's sake,
and then gave in.

' Don't think I've forgotten your crazy adventure
yesterday—but never mind ! Just remember not to
play about ; you're not still at pasture level up there.
But old Rödli will have his eye on you and he's tough
enough to throw you out if you don't behave your-
selves.'

' Of course we will, Father ! And if there are lots
of climbers in the hut we'll share a bunk, won't we,
Larry ? Or else we'll doss down on a bench in the
common-room—we're not fussy.'

They didn't take long getting ready ; they put on
thick shirts, corduroy trousers and heavy mountain
boots, and they each stuffed a couple of jerseys into
their rucksacks, for up there the nights would be cold.
They also took with them a fresh two-pound cheese,
a slab of butter, some bacon and a packet of tea-bags—
' Godfather always needs provisions ! '

' You can pick up two loaves on your way through
Kandersteg—there's never enough bread. What

81

about some packets of soup and smoked sausage, too ? '

' Yes, yes, Mother, don't fuss, we'll manage ! We're not going away for a month, you know ! '

Father Gruber checked each rucksack to make sure that nothing was missing, and seized the opportunity to remove the field-glasses that Peter had slipped in surreptitiously.

' Can you beat it ! I thought you'd try to get away with these. Rödli has a pair, in any case. You'll just have to fight it out with him.'

Peter protested, but in vain, and he had to leave the glasses behind. He consoled himself by the prospect of sneaking the pair in the hut, for they would need glasses in order to watch the climbers. ' Come on, Larry, let's make a start. It's nine o'clock and we've a good way to go : two hours to Kandersteg, half an hour for shopping—we'll drop in on your parents, too, if they're at home—and a five hours' climb up to the hut. No time to waste ! '

Goodbyes were said all round, with last-minute advice to the boys, which they did not heed, for they were already striding across the pasture. When they reached the copse they turned to wave, then started off down the path leading to the valley. They were in fine form and kept up a good pace, taking long strides, cutting corners wherever they could and jumping over the rushing streams in their deep rocky beds.

In what seemed a very short time they reached the

valley. At the first sight of the village houses, Larry was taken aback ; after spending three weeks high up in the enclosed world of mountain pasture, he had almost forgotten that there *were* any other people ! Everything seemed strange—the cars, the shoppers in the high street, the little church and the big hotels. The two boys came to a halt in the market-square.

' Do you see the Golitschenalp, Larry—that green slope high up above us ? And the chalet—that tiny little dot ? It looks as if it's standing just under the ridge. Come on now, let's hurry up and do our shopping, then we'll go and see if your parents are at home.'

But the Grubers' house, which Larry's parents rented for the holidays, was empty. No one came to answer their knock, though a neighbour appeared.

' Hullo ! It's Peterkin and the little Alsatian boy ! '

' Good morning, Madame Kramer. Isn't anyone at home ? '

' Goodness, no, not in fine weather like this ! They took the earliest cable-car up to the Stock mountain : they meant to go as far as the Gemmi col, I know.'

' I see ! Please will you tell them that we called, Madame Kramer, and that we are going up to my godfather's hut ? '

' Yes, of course, I'll tell them—they'll be so pleased. Give old Rödli my best wishes ! '

The boys didn't dawdle any longer but settled their

rucksacks and strode off in the direction of the chair
lift station.

'We shall gain an hour if we take the chair lift to
the Oschinen lake,' decided Peter, 'and that will be
something. We shall have quite enough climbing to
do later on, believe you me.'

They were lucky; there weren't many people at the
station, and one of the first little lifts—double-seated
chairs firmly hitched to a cable by a steel rod—carried
them high up above the tops of the pine-trees.

'It's terrific, Peter—look, the village is getting
smaller and smaller, as if it's sinking into a hollow!
There's Golitschen—and the Almen—and old Harry's

hut out on the mountain pasture. But it's queer to be
hanging in space like this—it gives me the shivers ! '

Peter laughed.

' Yes, we're twenty metres or so above the mountain-
side, but it feels as if we're directly over the valley.
It's better to look up, not down.'

As they rose higher and higher the scenery became
grander, as if the stage were gradually being set, while
at their feet the dark pine forests subsided into the
valley. An entirely new world opened before them, a
world of glaciers, frozen snow and dizzy peaks, seen
at close range, as if almost within reach of their hands.

' Now we really *are* high up ! ' thought Larry.

When they had left the chair lift and were walking
along by the Oschinen lake, which lay embedded like
an emerald in its rocky setting, Larry couldn't take his
eyes off the peaks surrounding them on all sides. He
even had to tilt his head a little to see them properly,
they were so close : he recognised them vaguely, by
their positions, for there was a great difference between
this view and that seen from the Golitschenalp. What
he had supposed from far away to be a single unbroken
ridge turned out to be a huge concourse of rocks, where,
from higher up still, the glacier *séracs*, or ice-pinnacles,
came crumbling down. What had looked like smooth
unbroken snowfields turned out at close quarters to be a
fantastic accumulation of rocks, moraines, blocks of
ice and piles of snow.

They crossed a little wood of arrolla pines and rhododendron bushes glowing with brilliant flowers and reached the opening of a wide couloir leading straight to the Schneehorn glacier.

'We're going to climb up there,' explained Peter. 'The couloir looks pretty steep, but it's not as bad as it looks, you'll see. Once we've started it'll go like clockwork. The path winds, following the easiest gradients. Look up there! You can see the hut already—out on the shelf between those two glacier strips.'

'Where? I can't see anything.'

'Try again. Take the left side of the glacier, and follow it up as far as the moraine, that high block. The hut's just there—you can see a tiny little square. Have you got it now?'

'Yes, I see. What's that beside it?'

'That's the flag, fluttering in the wind.'

'Gosh, it's high enough!'

'You can say that again! There's a difference of more than a thousand metres between it and the lake. We'll be there in another three hours. When we reach the waterfall, a little higher up, we'll stop and have a bite—we'll be in the shade there. Come on, let's get moving.'

The waterfall came tumbling down from a tremendous height within a crevice of the rock, then the water coursed along a kind of canal formed by erosion, flowing towards the lake. Two thick planks set side by side on flat pieces of rock made it possible to cross the rushing stream. Here the boys came to a stop. The air was full of invisible drops of water, refreshing and delightful.

Larry was only too glad to unbuckle his heavy rucksack, for he was hungry and thirsty. They ate and drank frugally, in the way of mountain-dwellers: a piece of sausage, a slice of bread, a few raisins and some cold tea.

'Remember this, Larry: don't eat or drink too much *en route*—it's a sound principle.'

'You're like a professor, with your principles! I'm hungry and I want to quench my thirst. Give me the bottle!'

'Nothing doing! You'd never stay the course, believe me. Your legs would simply fold up and we'd have to turn back. We'll never get there if you stuff yourself and drink your fill. Anyway, time's up. If we stop too long, we'll lose speed: we should need another half-hour to get back into training. If you're ready, we'll be on our way.'

'All right, you old skinflint! Keep your food and drink! I'm ready for anything—let's go!'

## 10

## *Surprise for Peter*

Poor Larry! He never knew how he managed the
last part of the climb or how he reached the hut
eventually, for during the last half-hour he was no
longer conscious of anything around him. He struggled
through the lower glacier séracs without even looking
at them, absorbed as he was in fighting his fatigue
and almost total exhaustion, which took all his will-
power.

Even Peter looked pale and gritted his teeth, but
carried on imperturbably at the same slow steady pace,
leading his friend to the Swiss Alpine Club's hut.

It had taken them a good three hours to climb
the couloir. To begin with, after their pause for a
snack, all went well. They chatted a little, not much
however, for in spite of Peter's claims, the climb was
steep enough to force Larry to save his breath.

Not far from the waterfall, they met two roped
climbers coming down, burnt brown by the sun,
drunk with happiness and fatigue. It did not matter
that these two were grown men, while they were boys,

or that they were strangers ; all four exchanged
laughing friendly greetings, for they were all mountaineers, two coming up and two going down, joined in a
common bond of fellowship.

Half-way up the boys waved vigorously to warn
Peter's godfather of their coming. He was usually
on the look-out, field-glasses at the ready, to catch sight
of anyone approaching the hut. After this their
enthusiasm gradually subsided. Their rucksacks
became heavier, their muscles stiffened and they grew
short of breath. At the foot of the steep rock wall
joining the couloir to the glacier they paused. They
had to circle this wall by means of a narrow ledge with
a frightening drop beneath, and Peter decided that they
needed a moment's rest before tackling it, in spite of
the steel rope fastened to pitons, which eased the way.

'Be very careful here,' he said to Larry. 'Hold on
to the rope with both hands, face the rock and keep as
close to it as you can—and you'll be all right.'

They had to make three similar trips before reaching
the base of the huge kidney-shaped rock on which the
hut stood. Here Larry noticed a tablet tucked into a
niche, saying *Schneehorn Hut—15 minutes*, and heaved
a great sigh, which made them both laugh—but those
fifteen minutes were the worst of all.

Larry thought he'd never make it, yet in the end he
did, and he now sat slumped on a bench in the common-
room, with no energy left even to take off his rucksack,

89

staring vacantly in front of him with his chin on his hands, dead-tired, beyond caring.

Father Rödli had welcomed them warmly, his face creased with smiles, and had immediately put on some water to boil for tea. It amused him to see them dressed up like real mountaineers yet worn out like children.

' Well, well, my boys, the climb up to the Schnee-horn seems to have been too much for you ! You must eat something—a sugar lump or two first of all—and you'll find some prunes in that tin, Peter. Then you must have a hot drink, and you'll feel better.'

Larry gradually felt the strength coming back to his legs and the tightness leaving his chest, and he began to take notice of his surroundings. Peter had already emptied their bags : their jerseys lay on the lower bunk they would share that night ; the food they had brought was stored in the baskets provided for that purpose. Father Rödli was delighted with the pro-visions—he was only sorry they hadn't brought any tobacco, for he had just enough left for one or two more pipes.

' Never mind ! I'm sure there'll be someone else coming up this evening who'll bring me a packet.'

Seated at the rough wooden table, hands behind their heads and legs outstretched, the two boys savoured the bliss of a meal well earned. Larry was very happy. For the first time he felt the thrill of real achievement and of using his strength to the utmost.

'You know, Peter, it wasn't the length of the climb so much as the difficult going.'

'Yes, it's a stiff climb, no doubt about that, but isn't this grand ? Don't you feel good now ? '

'I certainly do ! I'd never have believed it could be so wonderful to sit still.'

'Just wait and see how soundly you'll sleep tonight.'

'I'm sure I shall,' Larry answered, laughing. 'I'm already looking forward to it. Isn't the hut super ? You'd never expect it here, 2500 metres up.'

'Actually, it's 2540. Yes, it's grand here, just as it is in all the other huts. There's room for twenty-four climbers, you know. Of course it's a bit crowded when it's full, but that doesn't often happen—mostly only on a Saturday night in the height of the season.'

'It doesn't look as if anyone else's coming today. We're on our own, which seems a pity ! '

'It's a bit early still. The roped parties wouldn't get here till this evening. Don't worry ; it's such a fine day, someone's sure to come.'

Just at this moment they heard someone moving about on the floor above, and then the sound of steps.

'Well, it looks as if there's someone here already,' said Peter.

A girl appeared, coming down the stairs : she was about thirteen or fourteen years old, with brown hair crowned by a woolly cap with a pompom, and a slim figure. She moved briskly, and was dressed like a boy

91

in a red flannel shirt, trousers and thick woollen stock-
ings.

Larry looked at her full of curiosity, thinking:
'What on earth is she doing here?' But Peter had
already sprung forward.

'Gosh, I didn't know you were here!'

'Are you surprised to see me, Peter? I've been with
Grandfather for over a week.'

In the tiny kitchen old Rödli was rocking with
laughter. He put his head in at the door.

'You'd no idea, had you, Peter? It's a real surprise!'
He added teasingly: 'I quite forgot to say anything
about it.'

Peter blushed, like a little boy caught red-handed,
and stammered something; he really was overcome
with surprise.

Larry found it very good fun, and cast a quizzical
eye at his friend, thinking: 'I never saw Peter shy
before—blushing like that too!'

'Is this your friend, Peter?' asked the girl.

'Yes, this is Larry. He's spending the holidays on
the Golitschen with us,' said Peter, and then, turning
to Larry: 'This is my second cousin, Margaret—
call her Gretel—she comes from Frutigen. If only
I'd known!'

Peter was still nonplussed, and the three stared
solemnly at each other for a while, until Larry, who
could bear it no longer, burst out laughing. This

broke the ice ; the others joined in and soon they were all sitting on the bench together, the girl between the boys, talking away a mile a minute. They quickly became good friends and Peter suggested : ' Let's go out. You must at least have a look at the mountains, Larry, now that we're rested.'

Father Rödli's voice called out : ' Put on your jerseys, boys ! It's cold outside.'

All three crowded on to the bench set against the wall of the hut, in full sunlight. Although they were sheltered from the wind they could hear it whistling and wailing round the nearest peaks with a strange monotonous piercing sound, full of weird laments, like music from another world—a world of icy, inhuman solitude, with steep slopes, soaring peaks and frozen snow, all sparkling in the dazzling light.

Peter began naming the various peaks : furthest to the left lay the queen of the range, the Blümlisalp, then the Oschinenhorn, with its dangerous north wall, the Schneehorn, towering above the hut, and to the right, half-hidden behind the long Galletgrat ridge, the lovely Doldenhorn pyramid, with its twin snow-capped peaks.

Opposite them, at the threshold of the hut, the Schneehorn glacier climbed to the heights of the col, where drifts of iridescent snow whirled in the wind.

' The climb was worth it, wasn't it ?' asked Peter.

' I should say so ! This is worth everything.'

They sat basking in the sun for some time, leaning against the hut's warm stone wall and swinging their legs. Occasionally Larry took an inquisitive look at Gretel, who didn't seem at all shy of the boys on either side of her. It was true that she'd known Peter for a long time, and Larry for his part had never made anyone feel shy. She took an active share in their conversation, for she knew every bit as much about the mountains as her cousin. Her eyes shone, and it was easy to see that she was pleased to have companions of her own age. It was not that she had found life boring, what with the constant coming and going of the roped climbers, the evening bustle when everyone gathered round the common-room table in the atmosphere of warmth and friendliness that mountaineering engenders, and the constant thrill of the mountains themselves. But as she couldn't leave the hut she was often alone for hours together, so that the arrival of the two boys was a real godsend to her.

' She looks nice,' thought Larry, ' even though she does seem rather bossy. She won't be a nuisance and I think we'll all get on well.'

Peter had embarked on a long explanation for his friend's benefit, telling him how the hut got its supplies, especially firewood for heating, which was delivered by a helicopter that landed on the glacier, and how the mountain rescue service was organised. Occasionally Gretel would put in a word, giving up-to-date news of the hut and of the climbing expeditions of the last few days.

They would have lingered chatting together longer still if they had not been interrupted by the sound of light-hearted yodelling from the foot of the moraine. They rushed forward to see that was happening.

'There you are, Larry! Here come the first roped climbers!'

## 11

## *First Night at the Hut*

They could see three men, about ten minutes away from the hut, slowly climbing the path. Peter stood up straight and answered them with the echoing yodels of which he knew the secret. The leader stopped and waved his hand vigorously.

' I think it's Georg, Rudi Saax's brother, with two clients,' said Peter. ' Yes, I'm sure it is ! This is going to be fun ! '

The climbers had reached the last lap and could be seen clearly now. They seemed to be heavily laden and the ice-axes fastened to their rucksacks rose above their heads like strange antennae. They were certainly glad to reach the end of their journey and their arrival was tumultuous, for although his clients, two strong silent Englishmen, settled down peacefully enough, Georg Saax made so much commotion that he seemed to fill the whole hut to overflowing. As soon as he was inside the door, he showered Peter with punches by way of greeting, thumped Rödli on the shoulders and tossed him a packet of tobacco, stirred up the fire without even taking off his rucksack, and then embarked on a lively conversation with the keeper while he unpacked his belongings, giving him news from the village, forecasting the weather and describing previous climbs to the accompaniment of dramatic gestures. It was like having twenty people in the hut.

The two Englishmen had quietly made themselves at home meanwhile, choosing their bunks, inspecting the kitchen and stowing away their bags, and were now sitting at the table in a corner, enjoying their first pipe after the climb.

The three friends were keenly watching the disposal of the ropes. Peter went up to the guide and asked : ' I say, Georg, may I coil your ropes ? '

' Coil my ropes ! Tangle them, you mean ! Oh, well, here you are ! Look out you don't twist even a thread, or you'll catch it ! '

Peter was thrilled and settled down on one of the benches to coil the supple nylon rope with the care and concentration of a seasoned climber. It wasn't an easy task and Larry admired his skill.

' That rope isn't very thick ! I shouldn't feel too safe if I were fastened to it.'

' To begin with, you aren't " fastened to it " ! It's simply there to give you confidence, you know— that's all that matters. Of course, it can save you from falling and put the brakes on a skid, but you ought to climb as if there were no rope at all. If you do stumble or trip up, the chap in front will hold you fast ; if the worst comes to the worst, you'll hang on the rope, and believe me, the rope will bear you ! It's made to stand a weight of up to 1500 kilos, so you can see . . .'

Georg, who was writing his clients' names in the hut's big register, began to laugh.

' Have you quite finished giving us all a lesson ? We've certainly heard enough ! Mind you don't touch the rappel rope ; I'll deal with that myself.'

' Oh, all right ! But why do you need a rappel rope—where are you going ? '

' We're climbing the Ostgrat.'

' The Ostgrat ! ' exclaimed Peter, with a whistle of admiration that spoke volumes for the stiffness of the climb. ' You're not serious ! '

' Why not ? It must be climbed sometimes ! And those two over there may not talk much but they're tough—I've tested them. We've done some climbing almost everywhere together and I think it'll be all right. We'll make it. If the weather holds it ought to be a grand climb. I haven't done it yet this year and I can't wait ! '

From outside came the sound of the door banging, shoes being knocked against the wall to free them of snow, and ice-axes being hung up on their rack, and two newcomers entered with a hearty ' Good evening all ! ' They came into a welcoming atmosphere. It did not matter that no one knew each other, nor even spoke

* Kilo is an abbreviation of kilogram. One kilogram is 2.204 pounds.

99

the same language, for in the mountains people make friends immediately and wholeheartedly, sharing the same problems and the same pleasures, bound together as they are by their mutual passion for the mountains themselves. This passion forms their character and forges their friendships. A roped climbing party is far more than a team : its members are one in spirit, heart and will ; the pleasure and pain of each becomes that of all. Each man knows that the success of the next day's climb will be due to the effort and the will of all, that his own separate pleasure will depend on the rest and that his own life may very likely be in the hands of his roped companions. Together they will reach the summit, far from the valley and from human habitation, far away from the grey ordinariness of daily life, and together they will experience the thrill of those solitary heights.

Larry could read all this in the faces of those round him and could sense it in the warm-hearted atmosphere of the hut.

That evening there were fifteen seated round the rough tables, sharing the friendly meal. The company had been joined by several newcomers, two from Basle, who had been climbing for a fortnight, going from hut to hut, two Frenchmen and a Frenchwoman, and a team from Geneva.

Gretel had been busy setting the tables. Each group had handed Father Rödli a packet of soup and he, as chef, had hurled everything pell-mell into one sauce-pan, in defiance of all the rules of cooking—concentrated extracts of beef, onion, asparagus, mushroom and vegetable soup. The result was a good thick brew that everyone enjoyed, with the addition of thin slices of gruyère cheese. They also ate some bacon and drank huge bowls of tea, and dinner was over.

Everyone then settled down comfortably, some lighting pipes, and some fat Swiss cigars. Maps were spread out and itineraries studied : people discussed the best ways of approach, the difficulties of various slopes, how to get round séracs and climb *rimayes*, while Father Rödli stoked his fire and made it crackle cheerfully.

The conversation was general and everyone shared in it, sometimes resorting to gestures if the language barrier made this necessary ; people went from table to table, describing their plans for the morrow and exchanging tips and good advice.

Larry sat drinking it all in. Peter for his part kept interrupting, asking for explanations and demanding details. He wanted to know everything and he amused them all by his keenness. Georg spoke of his brother, Rudi : he hadn't seen him for several days and suspected that he was prowling about in the Golitschen area, it having been rumoured that the chamois were to be found there. Peter then told Georg what had happened the day before and repeated to him what

Rudi had said. Gretel and her grandfather had joined them and the five made a little separate group in a corner of the room.

' I don't know what's the matter with him,' said Georg. ' He's changed. He did give me an inkling, but I'd no idea things had reached such a pitch.'

' You must keep an eye on him,' Rödli put in. ' He's capable of doing something foolish. You know how obstinate he is ! '

' I do ! I think I'll get him to come along with me one of these days. We'll climb the Lohner peaks or something like that, and he'll just have to keep going. This chamois story is ridiculous ! '

' Be careful though—Rudi is a good chap but . . .'

' Well, we'll see ! Come on, Rödli, let's go outside for a minute to see how the wind blows—and then to bed ! '

Nearly everyone followed, for they were all hoping for fine weather, and the night sky often shows what morning will bring. They remembered to put on their heavy woollen jerkins, for it was very cold outside.

Darkness had eclipsed the mountain peaks, while a pale greenish light, which seemed to spring from the heart of the glacier, played on the slopes just below them. The sky was spangled with stars.

' It's bitterly cold ! ' cried Georg. ' It's sure to be fine tomorrow.'

' Hmm ! ' said Rödli. ' It'll be fine all right during

the day, but better not risk having to camp anywhere.'

' Is that what you think ? '

' Take my advice ! There's the hint of a *foehn* wind up there which will blow no one any good. But you're safe for the daytime at any rate ! '

They all hurried back to the cosy warmth of the hut and began giving Rödli their instructions for the morning : some of them were climbing the Doldenhorn and planned to leave at four o'clock. Georg and his two clients wanted to be waked at two because of the length and stiffness of the climb before them. The Schneehorn party were in no great hurry and only needed to get up at five.

Plans were soon fixed and all preparations made : rucksacks stood packed and ready as if on parade, ropes were coiled and ice crampons were firmly fastened to the rucksacks.

As soon as the light was put out Larry fell fast asleep. Around him there was still some movement as the sleepers got into a comfortable position for their short night, then silence fell. Only the wind, the mountain wind that never dies, pursued its restless course in the midst of the darkness and the solitude outside.

## 12

## Rudi Again

The boys were awakened at four by the comings and goings of the climbers in the hut. Georg and his roped party had already been gone some time. Squatting at the foot of their bunks, wrapped in blankets and still drowsy with sleep, the two friends watched the preparations.

The relaxed cheerful atmosphere of the evening before had vanished. The men ate quickly, while they went on getting ready, making a final check of the ropes and crampon bindings and putting on their anoraks and mufflers in almost total silence. It was easy to see that they were tense and excited. Their faces, which still bore traces of sleep, were slightly screwed up, as if each were hugging to himself some secret fear. High on the mountains, challenge and adventure awaited them, and in spite of their delight in this they could not escape the chilling atmosphere surrounding their departure in the bitterly cold and hostile small hours of the morning. Once outside, at grips with rock and ice, and especially when the first light of dawn broke over the slopes, things would seem different : fears and apprehensions would vanish, giving way to the joys and fellowship of the roped climb.

The hut had emptied by the time the boys at last decided to leave their bunk. Gretel, who slept upstairs in the keeper's room, hadn't yet come down ; Father Rödli was putting away the breakfast dishes.

' The sun is just rising, Larry ! Let's go and see ! It can be a wonderful sight.'

Although they had put on their two jerseys and mufflers and pulled their woollen caps down over their ears, the bitter cold gave them a shock.

' Brr ! It's absolutely freezing ! '

' It's always like this at dawn. It must be a few degrees below zero. Just listen to the wind ! '

It was blowing strongly through the wide gap made by the glacier between the Galletgrat and the Schneehorn ; it whistled along the ridges, sounding in the pale dawn like inhuman and sinister music, which made them shudder. The icy peaks gradually became clearer and a faint light suffused the eastern sky ; the Rothhorn ridge was like a mauve streak in the slowly kindling scene.

And then the miracle happened.

Above the dark valleys the sky took on a green hue which seemed to drive the night back into its own darkness : brilliant orange horizontal stripes spread

across this background and the fluffy domed clouds
crowning the Blümlisalp burst into flame.

It was a fairyland of colour, as if the whole sky were
on fire. The frozen snow on the eastward-facing
heights was lit up, and the Morgenhorn snow-cornice
reflected a dazzling beam of light.

' It's magnificent, Peter ! It's far more beautiful
than any sunset ! '

' Yes, that's true enough ; it's wonderfully beautiful,
but they aren't usually very pleased to see it in these
parts. It isn't a good omen, and I think Godfather
was right yesterday evening when he foretold that the
fine weather wouldn't last. But let's go in ! My teeth
are chattering and I'm beginning to feel hungry.'

A little later, when the sun had reached the hut,
they dug themselves in behind the woodpile ; here
Gretel joined them and they spend the whole morning
there together, leaning against the stripped pine logs,
following the climbers' progress through the field-
glasses.

The sky was now uniformly blue, with only a few
small clouds, or fish, as Peter called them, floating
about 3000 metres up. Visibility was excellent and
thanks to the glasses they could follow all the hazards
of the climbs.

Georg and his two Englishmen had vanished for
the time being among the chaos of the séracs, to
reappear much later for a moment above the dangerous

Ostgrat pillar, making for the Ostgrat ridge itself. The other roped parties were visible all morning : two were climbing the Schneehorn, while the French team was attacking the Galletgrat. The latter would not return to the hut ; once they had reached the summit they planned to go down to the Doldenhorn hut.

The tiny little figures were outlined against the slope. A roped party climbs very slowly.

'Apparently there are some really tricky bits in the Galletgrat climb,' Peter explained. 'They aren't going very fast but they're climbing well, and they're taking great care. Look! One behind the other, slow but sure!'

At one point they heard a clear tinkling sound like a chime of bells.

'What's that?' asked Larry.

'That's the leader driving in a piton—you know, those steel spikes with a ring that you saw yesterday evening. Those are pitons. He hammers them into tiny cracks in the rock-face. This usually means that it's stiff going and that there aren't many holds. Look, he's clinging to that straight pillar-like rock. I know that climbers usually avoid it; there's a short traverse that can be made just there, but probably they don't know about it, so they're going straight on. I must say, they're super climbers! The leader's terrific.'

Passing the glasses to and fro they shared the whole tricky operation, just as if they were part of the team. Sometimes there were long pauses, while the leader decided on his exact route, then the climbers would go ahead fast for two or three metres. The watchers could clearly see the rope passing through the hands of the second member of the team—the young woman, whom they recognised by the red cap—as she stood quite confidently on a narrow shelf.

'They've made it!' cried Peter. 'Look, the leader has reached the top of the spur. Now they've only got to follow the ridge. It's in the bag—in an hour they'll be at the summit.'

' What about the others on the Schneehorn ? How are they getting on ? Pass me the glasses.'

' They've taken their time to reach the frozen snow,' said Gretel. ' Yet it isn't supposed to be a difficult climb. There's quite a good slope.'

' Hmm, I know, but those Schneehorn rocks are always damp, you know, and they may have found them covered with verglas, and that certainly makes for dangerous going. You have to be careful not to slip and not to leave go, otherwise you may drag all the team down with you. That means that it's like tight-rope walking and you have to go very slowly, hardly touching the surface of the rock—almost like flying.'

' Anyway, they've managed it all right, for now they are on the frozen snow,' said Larry. ' The first team is well ahead.'

' It can't be easy, at that ! Watch the leader. He's having to cut steps with his ice-axe. The snow must be very hard, seeing how cold it was last night, and when it rained on the Golitschen the day before yesterday it must have been snowing up here. There's no sign of a path, so they have to cut their way. It takes ages and it's hard work ! '

It was already eleven o'clock when they saw the climbers reach the summit and disappear round the other side of the cornice.

' It's no use waiting any longer ! ' pronounced Peter.

' They'll be gone some time and we've lost sight of the Galletgrat party too. There's no more to be seen. Let's go in and have an early lunch if we can. I've got a plan—we must try and carry it out while it's still fine ! '

The other two bombarded him with questions but it was no use, Peter wouldn't breathe a word.

' No ! I'm not going to tell you a thing. As for you, Gretel, you're a girl and I don't even know if we can take you.'

' What awful cheek ! You dare leave me behind ! Why should you, anyway ? You can't possibly mean to climb the Ostgrat ! Where you can go, I can go, there's no doubt about that. And I shall, too, wherever it is.'

Peter burst out laughing.

' We'll see, if you're very good . . .'

' Oh, you're the limit ! '

The two chased each other round the hut, laughing and shrieking, till Peter finally rushed in at the open door with Gretel and Larry on his heels. They all stopped short on the common-room threshold, where a surprise awaited them.

Rudi sat there, smoking a pipe and talking to Father Rödli. They broke off their conversation abruptly when the three friends came in ; Rudi looked embarrassed, and Father Rödli got up mumbling into his beard. He had been scolding the young guide harshly.

There was an awkward silence for a moment or two. The two boys were confused and couldn't help thinking uncomfortably of the confidences Rudi had made them. As for Rudi himself, he was still feeling the effect of his talk with the keeper of the hut, and he had a surly look ; nevertheless, it was he who broke the silence.

' Hullo, you two ! '

' Hullo, Rudi ! '

' Hi, Gretel, are you here, too ? That makes it a real family gathering.'

He wasn't much in the mood for joking but he pulled himself together and added : ' Well, Peter, so you're not still keeping watch on the Golitschen ? Suppose I'd taken the opportunity to shoot the chamois ? '

' Oh, the chamois ! He must be miles away by now. He won't be back for ages.'

' You're absolutely right. That's why I'm here. There was nothing doing down there, and I heard that Georg had come up, so I thought I'd catch him on his way back. But Rödli tells me that he's climbing the Ostgrat, which means that he'll go down again by way of the Doldenhorn hut, so I'm out of luck. What about you—what are you doing here ? '

' Well, I wanted to show Larry the hut, and as I wasn't worried about the chamois any more . . .'

' He won't gain anything by waiting. I'll get him yet.'

' That's what you think. We'll see ! ' snapped Peter.

' There's no doubt about it.'

' Don't you believe it ! '

They were growing more and more annoyed and Peter's hackles were rising, so Rödli intervened :

' Peter, come over here a moment ! As you've nothing to do, start the fire for me. The others will soon be back and they'll kick up a fuss if the soup isn't ready.'

This calmed things down a little and while Larry ran to the wood-pile to get a fresh stock of logs Peter told his godfather what they planned to do that afternoon.

' Climb the Schneehorn ? What an idea ! You can't possibly get up to your tricks there. I don't mind if you play about in the fallen rocks to the right of the central couloir, but you're not to climb the Schneehorn proper ; do you understand ? '

' Of course, Godfather ! And we won't go very high. We'll stay in the rocks at the foot and climb about among them. You know it's not dangerous there.'

' No, not if you stay on that side of the couloir ! Anyway, it's quite simple : you know the first patch of snow reaching down into the big couloir ? Well, you can go as far as that, and I forbid you to go any further. Do you understand ? '

' Yes, Godfather, that's quite enough for us. We can have lots of fun there.'

Peter spoke perfectly sincerely. He had no intention of going any higher or of tackling the rock-face itself, but he did not realise that the best resolutions melt like snow in summer before the challenge of adventure.

## 13

## As far as the Patch of Snow

The two roped Schneehorn parties returned about one o'clock, almost at the same time. The five men were exhausted, but this didn't prevent them from describing their feat at the tops of their voices, with a great many dramatic gestures.

' We're worn out. I've never known the snow so hard. As for the rocks, you never saw anything like it —they're covered with verglas. We couldn't get a decent hold anywhere.'

' I don't know how we managed to climb—but we did ! We pulled it off somehow, and it was really marvellous ! '

Rudi joined in the conversation, sucking away at his short pipe, and they discussed the various routes, the problem of verglas and the atmospheric conditions.

' Well, Rödli, what about that soup, eh ? We're as hungry as hunters.'

' Here you are—soup coming up.'

' I haven't brought any contributions,' explained

Rudi. ' I meant to share Georg's lunch, but now that
he's going down by way of the Doldenhorn . . .'

' Don't worry, it doesn't matter a bit. There's
plenty for everyone. Come on, fall to ! '

The five men, their faces tanned by the mountain air
and the dazzling reflection from the frozen snow,
their eyes reddened but shining with excitement and
their hair tousled, began eagerly spooning up Father
Rödli's thick soup.

Peter, Larry and Gretel made haste to follow
their example. They had decided to start as soon as
the meal was over. Peter's godfather had assured
them that he didn't need their help with the washing-
up and as soon as they had swallowed their last mouth-
ful they hurried off, before he could change his mind.

' First of all we must traverse the left-hand side of
the glacier. There's nothing to it. There's no crevasse
on that side, we've only got to follow the track made
by the roped climbers this morning.'

They walked in single file, with Gretel in the middle,
just like a real roped team making an ascent. It was a
great thrill for Larry. He would never have believed
it possible for him to undertake such a climb so high
up in the mountains. The glacier itself was exciting
enough, with its crisp fresh snow that crunched under-
foot and the track they had to follow.

' Mind you keep close together,' said Peter, who led
the way. ' You never know what may happen ! '

116

He was taking his position as ' guide ' very seriously, giving them all kinds of advice, showing them how to put their feet down without slipping and explaining why the track wound now to the right, now to the left, according to the gradient.

' It's no use trying to forge straight ahead, it's too steep and too difficult.'

Just then a dull rumbling crack sounded on their right.

' Something's moving down there.  It's a crevasse opening wider, or a block of ice melting, but don't be frightened, we're in no danger.'

' We're not frightened, for Heaven's sake,' replied Larry.  ' Just get a move on—we're waiting to follow.'

The track now led straight to the central Schneehorn couloir.  Half an hour had passed since they left the hut.  In spite of the keen air they were sweating and Larry began to talk of shedding a jersey.

' You mustn't think of it !  You'd catch cold, especially now we're starting to sweat.  This is the end of our climb anyway, so we can rest for a bit.'

They were at the foot of the steep Schneehorn rockface, which they could now see was not quite perpendicular, as it had appeared to be from a distance, but sloped a little.

' Listen, Peter, it can't be that difficult to climb.  It's not at all steep.'

' No, it isn't, if the rock-face conditions are good ;

they say it's like a Sunday afternoon stroll. The traverse is almost like a path—everyone follows the same track, you see, so it's very well trodden. But don't let's stay here at the bottom of the couloir. We might easily be hit by a falling stone—we shouldn't have any warning.'

They moved away to the right, following the glacier for a hundred yards, and came face to face with a jumble of rocks.

'Here we are,' cried Peter. 'We can climb here quite safely, Godfather said we could. There's no need to be roped, none of the rocks are very big and we can practise scaling—but let's go up a little higher. We can, easily ; we'll scale a few of the bigger rocks on the way. Godfather said that we could go as far as the snow-patch in the couloir. It must be nearly 3000 metres high up there, and it's quite safe. There's a little five-metre chimney just before you come to the couloir, which it would be fun to climb.'

'All right, let's be on our way,' said Larry. 'I'd like to get up as high as I possibly can. I'm longing to see my parents' faces when I tell them that I've been climbing so high up.'

So Peter led his little 'team' across the fallen rocks. Naturally there was no path, especially as Schneehorn climbers usually followed the left side of the couloir and attacked the rock-face direct.

The three friends skirted the big rocks and amused

themselves by climbing several smaller rocks in turn. It was thrilling and not at all dangerous. They climbed gradually higher and higher, scaling one rock after another and helping each other as things got more difficult, until they reached the chimney Peter had told them about.

' What do you think of it, Larry ? It's a little like our Golitschengrat peak, but not nearly so tall—hardly five metres—although it's almost perpendicular, to make up for it. Shall we have a go ? What about you, Gretel—do you think you can manage it ? You'll have to concentrate, I warn you.'

' What a pair of show-offs ! Anyone would think you were experts, to hear you talk ! I've already told you, Peter, that I'll follow you wherever you go, so it's your look-out. Anyway, I'm just as well equipped as you, and I don't see why I shouldn't climb as well, too.'

' Calm down, Gretel, calm down ! I didn't mean to make you angry. This will be our adventure for today. I'll go first, then Gretel in the middle and Larry can bring up the rear. Full steam ahead to the couloir, then ! '

It certainly was ' fun ', as Peter had put it. The fissure was very deep but hardly more than three feet wide. It was as if they were climbing right inside the rock, and the enclosed feeling gave them a sense of complete security. There were plenty of

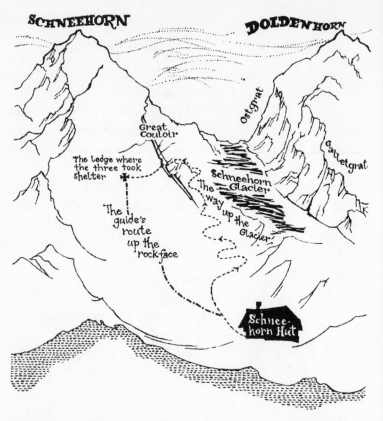

holds, the rock was solid and it seemed like child's play to the three 'Alpinists'.

They were young and active, lively and supple, which made up for the imprudence of scaling the chimney without being roped, unaccompanied by an experienced guide.

Peter felt vaguely guilty at leading his two friends beyond the bounds of prudence. He was quite aware that if one or other of them let go, a fall, with all its consequences, would be inevitable. But he simply couldn't resist taking the risk.

' They're both good climbers, after all,' he said to himself, ' and they're not afraid. That's what matters. There's no reason why they should let go. Anyway, this is the only dangerous part . . . and Godfather won't know anything about it. We've only got to bring it off.'

They reached the mouth of the chimney without any setbacks and found themselves on the wide ledge leading to the patch of snow in the couloir.

' We've made it ! ' cried Peter. ' We're here ! That's the snow-patch which Godfather gave us as our limit. I know we could have got here without climbing the chimney by taking the lower route, but this was much more fun, don't you think ? '

' You were right, Peter. It would have been a shame to miss this.'

As they spoke they approached the couloir, which grew narrower and steeper at this height, allowing the snow to accumulate. They could see traces of previous climbers, and footsteps still quite clearly marked leading from one side to the other.

' It looks as if someone's crossed this way. They must have come up through the fallen rocks, as we did, instead of climbing the rock-face. It's quite a long detour, but of course it's much easier. Rudi would say that it's " less stylish ", too.'

'Well, why shouldn't we cross here, then?' asked Larry.

Climbing the chimney had stimulated them; they were eager for more and ready to undertake the maddest adventure, ignorant as they were of real mountaineering.

'But Godfather told us not to go any further.'

'Oh! you know Grandfather!' put in Gretel. 'If we listened to him we'd never do anything! Of course, if you're afraid . . .'

'Afraid! Me?'

This inevitably put to flight the remains of Peter's native prudence. Larry played his part, too, in persuading him.

'Look, Peter, there's nothing to it. The track's already made and on the other side we only have to follow the overhang. It's absolutely straightforward. Your old razor-blade was far more complicated! I can't think why your godfather wouldn't allow it, anyway.'

'Because on the other side of the couloir we'll be on the Schneehorn rock-face and we ought not to climb that without being roped.'

'We *ought* not to, I know. But we shan't go far. Don't you see how there's almost a path along that ledge—it's very wide, even if there is a sheer drop to the left. We've only got to cling to the overhang and we'll be all right. I'd love to do a bit more climbing. It seems ridiculous not to, when we're so close.'

' All right then ! But look out when we're crossing the snow-patch. Keep to the tracks and lean towards the mountain-side. If you stumble you'll slip right down to the bottom. We'll go in single file. I'll cross first.'

Peter tested the snow carefully : it was firm and compact and the tracks were well marked. As he advanced he packed the snow again at each step, to make the traverse easier for the other two. With his right hand he leant on the icy mountain-side and kept his eyes fixed on the tracks, taking no notice of the huge drop to his left.

Luckily it was a short traverse, but when he reached the other side of the couloir he called out, rather nervously, to Larry:

' Your turn, now ! Pack the snow again, as I did. It will be easier for Gretel.'

' Don't worry about me—I'll manage ! ' she cried.

In fact she made the traverse very well, following Larry, and ignored the hand Peter held out to help her over the last lap.

' Leave me alone. I can make it by myself.'

Nevertheless, although they wouldn't have admitted it, each of them had been afraid. Their reactions betrayed them, when they were reunited. Peter looked pale and rubbed his hands together nervously ; Gretel began laughing in a forced kind of way, as if to give herself courage, and Larry whistled under his breath, his hands deep in his pockets, pretending to be unconcerned. None of them really behaved naturally.

' Now, what shall we do ? ' asked Peter.

' Why don't we go on a bit ? Let's try and find somewhere to sit. I should think we'd have a marvellous view over the valley if we climb to the end of this ledge.'

They set off in single file, with no other support. The ledge rose gently for about sixty yards and led them to an overhang.

' Well, that's that ! We can't go any further, it would be madness. We should have to get round the overhang and that's impossible without being roped.'

' You're right, Peter. Let's stop here. We're sheltered from the wind, the sun's shining and we can see the hut and the glacier—we can even see as far as Oschinen ! And I've climbed higher than 3000 metres, though it's only about 500 from the hut.'

' Quite enough too. We've done enough crazy things for one day. I only hope Godfather doesn't spot us through his glasses.'

' Of course he won't. We'll take shelter. This is a good spot. The rock-face is pretty damp, but if we squeeze in under the overhang we shall keep dry.'

All three of them were glad to have a break, for they had been through a good deal. They were perfectly placed, snuggled up together and well sheltered, and they had a wonderful view. They could take their time to plan their descent, they thought.

But already danger was threatening the three friends although they were blissfully unaware of it.

## 14

## Verglas

Meanwhile peace reigned in the hut.  The two roped
teams, after resting for an hour, had gone down to the
valley.  The five men concerned, who had met for the
first time on the Schneehorn ascent, were already
planning joint expeditions for the future—for the
mountains had cast their magic spell of comradeship
once more.

Only Rudi and Father Rödli were left in the hut.
The keeper had fallen into a doze beside his stove,
while Rudi sat on the bench, leaning against the wall
with his legs outstretched, smoking a meditative pipe.
He would have liked to doze too, if only he had not
been harassed by his gloomy thoughts.  To be in the
familiar surroundings of the hut, high on the mountain,
made him even more conscious of the torment that
afflicted him.  It was so terrible not to be able to climb
any more, and he couldn't bear the thought of giving
up the mountains, which were his livelihood and his
life.  For a man like him there was no excitement in
roaming the pastures or climbing to one or other of the

huts : for him the essence of the mountains, to which he had dedicated his life, lay in these noble heights—glaciers, frozen snow and magnificent crests soaring to the sky in windy solitude.

' It's all very well for people to try to talk me out of it—they don't know what it's like. I shan't be happy until I put a bullet through that cursed chamois—otherwise I might as well give up, for nothing else makes sense.'

Father Rödli gave a great yawn and stretched himself, interrupting Rudi's thoughts.

' I must have been dozing,' said the keeper.

' Is that what you call it ? You've been snoring loud enough to raise the roof.'

' Don't tease me, Rudi—I'm getting old, you know, and I need my siesta. I have to get up at unearthly hours to wake all these chaps, and I'm not as good at it as I used to be, so I have to make up for it in the daytime.'

' Ah well, that's how it is, that's life.'

The two of them began philosophising, telling each other how quickly time flies, and the old keeper made a fresh attack on the guide, scolding him and openly taunting him, trying to persuade him to undertake a proper climb once more.

' It's all very fine for you to talk, Rödli. Words aren't any use, they don't help a bit. You'd much better poke your fire—it's beginning to feel chilly in here.'

127

' You're a fine one for talking, yourself. And what does it all amount to ? Why don't you shoot your chamois once and for all, and let's hear no more of it.'

' Do you think it's as simple as that ? I feel as if I'll never get him. Stop worrying about me, and stoke the fire. I'm freezing.'

' It's getting late, it's true. I don't think anyone will come up this evening. Look, there are clouds over the valley and the wind's blowing down from the mountain tops. The weather must be very bad at Kandersteg, and no one would start out in such conditions. I wonder where the children are, though ? They ought to be back. Will you spend tonight with us ? '

·' I'd like to, yes.'

' Good, that's fine. But what can they be up to ? It's six o'clock, and it'll soon be bitterly cold out there.'

' Wait a minute—I'll have a look.'

But from the threshold Rudi could see no one however far he looked. There was not a sign of the children on the moraine or the glacier, and although he raked the fallen rocks at the foot of the couloir with the field-glasses, there was nothing to be seen. He called the keeper.

' Hi, Rödli ! Come here a minute. I can't see them anywhere.'

' What's that ? They must be up there. And it's high time they were back. Just feel this wind ! Where can they have got to ?   What on earth are they doing ? '

The poor old man could not possibly have guessed what had happened to the three friends.

In fact, while he and Rudi were looking for them at the foot of the Schneehorn, they were still high up on the rock-face, crouched together under the over-hang, even though it was so late, wondering what would become of them.

They had spent a very happy hour to begin with, telling each other stories and jokes, and enjoying the wonderful view.   Then they had seen the clouds gathering over the lake and the distant valley, and the first veils of mist floating up the mountain-side, blotting out the pine-forests and forming a dense mass.   It was an amazing sight and they were fasci-nated.

Soon, however, the sun sank behind the Doldenhorn crest ;  the wind rose and although they were sheltered they felt its bite.   Cold comes very quickly on the mountains, as they discovered to their cost, for when Peter eventually decided to return, it was too late. As soon as he emerged from their natural shelter he started back in horror :  the rock-face, over which they had made their rash climb an hour before so gaily and light-heartedly, had become a menace.

' I knew something would happen to us ! '

' But what is it ?   What's the matter ? '

'Watch ! '   Peter took a step, holding firmly on to

129

the overhang above them—one tiny step, and his foot slipped. The rock was covered with verglas. In a bare ten minutes the cold had done its work.

It is well known that this side of the Schneehorn is damp all day long ; water falls slowly but continually, almost drop by drop, from the frozen snow up above, so that when it turns cold the whole rock-face is covered with a sheet of ice. The rash young climbers were caught in a trap.

' But we can't stay here ! ' protested Larry. ' We must go down at once.'

' Go down ? Just tell me how, Larry. We should have to break the ice with each step, and we simply couldn't do it. The tiniest slip would mean a fall, and there'd be nothing to cling on to with this cursed verglas. You realise what a fall could mean, with things as they are, don't you ? '

' What can we do then ? '

' Do ? Nothing. The only thing we can do is stay here, under the overhang. We're almost completely sheltered from the wind, if we take care and don't move about. We'll just have to wait—that's all we can do.'

' Wait ? But what for ? It's mad to think of spending the night here.'

' Yes, Larry, it probably is. We've got to face things. We can't possibly move ; remember what those chaps said when they got back this morning ? There's just nothing to be done. I hope there's someone in the hut ; Godfather will soon begin to worry. If only he can spy us through his field-glasses. We can't even make distress signals—it's too risky trying to move. Well, that's how it is ; we're in quite a good position, and he's bound to see us—perhaps he'll send a roped team to fetch us. Otherwise . . .'

' We'll have to spend the night here, won't we ? And that could be the end—we'd never survive.'

Peter was very pale but took a determined stand.

' We'll do the best we can. First of all, we must sit still and snuggle up close together so as to keep warm as long as possible. Look, I've still got a few prunes in my pocket. We'll share them and hope for the best.'

Peter was right to rely on his godfather : Rödli soon spotted them through his glasses and began to swear as no one had sworn in the hut before.

' Look at those idiots. Did you ever hear of anything so crazy ? They've actually crossed the couloir—do you hear that, they've crossed the couloir. They must be raving mad. It's Peter, of course—if only I had him here . . . And now they've squeezed themselves in under the overhang. Do you realise what's happened to them—yes, I suppose you do, because you know that rock-face as well as I do. The verglas has trapped them. And to think that I let them go ! Oh Rudi, Rudi, what are we going to do ? '

131

The guide in his turn had spotted the little group.

'Yes, Rödli, there they are under the overhang. There's no doubt about the verglas—it's not surprising in this cold. If only they don't move! But Peter's bound to realise that there's nothing for it but to wait.'

'But what can we do, Rudi? We can't leave them there—they'd never survive. We must send word to the valley and get hold of a rescue team. They simply can't spend the night up there.'

'No, that's definite. They must be got out of there, they must be rescued.'

The guide had slumped down on to the bench, his head in his hands. Rödli didn't even look at him but stormed on without taking his eyes off the rock-face.

' They're well over five hundred metres above the glacier. . .'

Suddenly Rudi got up.

' Listen, Rödli—I'll go.'

' What's that ? '

' I'll go, I tell you. What's so surprising about it ? It's the only way, and I'm a guide after all.'

' But, Rudi, wouldn't it be better to fetch a team from the valley ? '

' That's no use. You know perfectly well that there's not a minute to lose. Anything might happen to them. Help me to get ready, Rödli. I'm off.'

Like someone possessed, staring in front of him and moving as if on strings, he began equipping himself, jerking out orders abruptly as he did so.

' Two thermos flasks of piping hot tea. Be as quick as you can. Get out the belay rope and the *rappei* rope. Pass me all the jerseys the children have got. Stuff everything into your rucksack. No, I don't want any pitons—that'll be all we'll need.'

Without speaking and with a heavy heart, Father Rödli busied himself getting things together, knowing from long experience just what was needed. The two men understood each other almost without words, and in a quarter of an hour Rudi was ready : rucksack filled, ropes carefully coiled and fixed, the hood of his anorak pulled well down. Rödli went outside with him.

' Will you go round by the fallen rocks on the right ? '

' No, that's impossible.  I should have to cross the snow-patch in the couloir and with this verglas and no crampons it's too risky ;  it just *might* come off, but it would take too long.  There's no time to lose—I'm going straight up.'

' Will you be all right ? '

' I'll be all right, Rödli.  Either I make it—or I don't.  It's the acid test, isn't it ? '

' Rudi . . .'

' Yes ? '

' You *must* make it.  You *must* bring them back.'

' Don't worry.  Just get a roaring fire ready for us to come home to.  Goodbye.'

' Goodbye ! '

Rudi set off rapidly in the gathering dusk down the path leading to the glacier.  Rödli, desperately anxious, could not help wondering, after all that the guide had told him, whether Rudi would be able to overcome his mysterious weakness.

## 15

## *Rudi's Last Chance*

If the three had known that help was coming it would have comforted them, for they were desperate.

At the outset, only Peter realised exactly what had happened. Larry always had to put his oar in, but he was not seriously alarmed, for at heart he was sure that Peter would find a way of rescuing them. As for Gretel, she had said nothing. In fact she was highly entertained, seeing herself the heroine and the boys the heroes of a wonderful adventure which she could boast about to her girl-friends in Frutigen. It wasn't so terrible, after all, she thought, just a tiresome setback which would soon be over. It is so difficult to realise that something serious can happen to *us*—such things only happen to other people.

Gradually, however, they were forced to realise that their situation was desperate. Snuggled up together in the overhang's precarious shelter, they felt the cold gradually taking hold of them. The single jersey they had each pulled over their flannel shirts was not enough protection.

'Move your feet, wriggle your toes all the time, otherwise ... Don't leave your hands exposed!'

They squeezed closer and closer together as the cold grew sharper, feeling as if their bodies were turning to ice. Peter wanted to stand up, even though there was hardly room, to try to bring back some warmth by movement, but the wind seemed to pierce him and it took away his breath. Finally, when a livid light filled the sky and the sea of clouds vanished into the darkness reigning over the valley, while the wind's shrill keening rose to a higher key, they understood that they were lost.

Gretel had forgotten all about her girl-friends in Frutigen now. Sheltered to some extent by the boys on either side of her, she was crying quietly, tired to death, abandoning herself to her fate. Larry was shivering violently as the cold seized hold of his legs; he could feel icy fingers clutching at his heart and he was terrified. Peter alone, whose resistance was greater than that of his two friends, kept his head, weighing their chances of escape.

' It's such a stupid way to die—it just can't happen like this. It would be better to risk the descent. No, they must be getting worried at the hut—they'll send a roped team to rescue us. But supposing no one's there? In this awful weather . . . Don't panic! God-father will know what to do. He won't abandon us.'

If he had only known that Rudi was on his way it would have put fresh heart into him, but still he would not have felt absolutely sure of their being rescued, remembering the guide's confession and his fatal hesitation on the rock that day. Moreover, with conditions as bad as they were . . .

Rudi, too, was far from certain that he would succeed. The decision that he had taken almost instinctively, his honour as a man and as a guide being at stake, and the driving energy of his departure were forgotten now that he stood at the foot of the rock-face.

' I acted too quickly,' he said to himself, ' far too quickly. But what else could I do ? '

To begin with the going was easy, for he only had to make his way through fallen rocks, both large and small ; but when he reached the slab marking the beginning of the ascent proper he stopped dead. Leaning his forehead against the stone and clasping it with both hands he could feel his heart beating with heavy thuds, and he tried to cheer himself up.

' Good Heavens, I know this—it's only the little Schneehorn slab ! It's as easy as pie. The fissure crosses it diagonally—there's nothing to it.'

Mentally he reviewed the ascent, which he had made so often and which he could once have done with his eyes shut.

' The slab first, then the little dihedral ; then the long traverse, then the fissure, then the chimney, and that ought to bring me almost to the children. There's no need to get the wind up—I've simply got to get going.' Slowly and determinedly he put all thoughts out of his head, even those of the climb, and set himself to make the ascent.

The slab was damp, but he didn't worry about that. There was a diagonal crack crossing it, wide enough for a foothold : it was only necessary to find a hand-hold from time to time, and progress wasn't difficult.

After five minutes he came to the foot of the dihedral and leant up against the rock in the angle of its two planes. But when he was about to turn round to face the rock he felt his heart come into his mouth and without any warning a terrible anguish seized him. His limbs became heavy as lead, huge drops of sweat broke out on his forehead and he seemed to see the chamois waiting for him, staring at him with burning eyes, daring him to go any further.

Rudi flung himself against the rock, mad with fright, and stayed there for a long time, panting and trembling, waiting panic-stricken for the terrible giddiness, that had defeated all his other attempts, to overtake him. The same thing was happening— it would always be the same.

'No, it isn't the same. This time the children are up there, and if I don't get to them, they'll be lost.'

Then with unutterable joy he found himself growing fiercely, irresistibly angry, and he knew that he was cured. Full of confidence now, he pitted his strength against the rock, seizing hold of it fiercely, stamping his feet and shouting out the coarsest oaths ever mouthed by an Oberland mountaineer. Anger isn't usually a good counsellor; but nothing else could have given him the courage to revenge himself against the chamois.

Without waiting any longer, Rudi launched his attack on the dihedral, shaking his fist challengingly. Taking a firm grip of the fissure, one foot on either side of the two planes of rock, he climbed methodically, without a single surplus movement but with surprising speed. There was no verglas yet, except in odd spots where it didn't worry him.

All the same, the way he rushed at the climb betrayed his uneasiness, and his feverish excitement was surely due to his longing to escape from the anguish that tortured him. He must have been wondering if he would ever recapture the ease and security which had made him one of the best guides in the neighbourhood—in fact, if he would ever find himself again.

After a climb as long as a normal length of rope he would reach the traverse. But the exit from the dihedral was tricky : one of the rock-walls seemed to bear down abruptly, a slight overhang almost blocked the fissure and for nearly two yards the climb had to be made with scarcely any holds. For a seasoned climber like Rudi, it should have been child's play ; yet when he found himself hanging in space, his legs pressing horizontally against the overhang, one hand tucked into the narrow fissure and his body arched backwards, he felt panic-stricken again for a moment. 'I'll never make it,' he thought. And the chamois seemed to be there, waiting for him on the traverse.

He tried desperately to find a hold for his free left hand, but there were no notches in the damp smooth rock-face. A dark mist blinded him and he was on the point of letting go, giving up the struggle and falling down, down into space. Then with an angry movement and a terrible oath, he swung his body to the right, against the rock, thrust up his left hand and hooked himself on to the traverse above him by a razor-thin ledge. With the same spirit that had propelled him at the beginning he hung on to the miraculous hold like a limpet, hoisted his legs, thrust out his right hand and dragged himself up. He had made it.

Panting, exhausted and almost lying along the traverse, Rudi got his breath back slowly. His mind was a blank, he was completely taken up with the effort of controlling his jerky heart-beats and trembling hands. As he grew calmer, he began laughing at himself. ' I was climbing just like a beginner. Simply because I had no faith in myself. To think that I nearly didn't make it.'

Then he realised that during his desperate effort to reach the traverse he had not once thought of the chamois. He smiled briefly and at once began cursing himself, calling himself all kinds of names ; he felt the intolerable weight slipping from him and the de-vouring anguish leaving him, and knew that he was himself again. In one swift movement he pulled him-self together, adjusted the strap of his rucksack and attacked the traverse with a thunderous roar of laughter which echoed on the wind as far as the hut and up to the three children.

Peter got up suddenly, thinking he heard voices ;

he was afraid it was the wind playing tricks on him, but then again he seemed to hear something—someone laughing! He was sure of it now: there was someone on the rock-face below them.

'I say, there's a roped team down below. They're coming up, I'm sure. I heard them.'

His two friends, crouched under the rock, their knees drawn up under their chins, motionless and listless, did not reply, but a gleam came into their fever-bright eyes. They had heard something too, but they were unable to move. Peter, filled with excitement, felt hope rising in him once more and began shouting repeatedly for help, but his cries were borne away and lost on the wind.

Rudi heard nothing; he had already reached the fissure that rose above the traverse. It was growing darker and colder every minute and he had come across some verglas, but nothing could have stopped him now.

He attacked the fissure from the outside. He was no longer afraid but climbed with perfect ease, hardly seeming to touch the rock-face, making himself as light as a feather; his feet skimmed over the verglas and his hands had recovered all their sensitive touch, in spite of the cold benumbing them. He had taken off his mitts so that he could feel the rock better. Completely absorbed in his task, he did not let up for an instant, wholeheartedly enjoying his solitary climb in spite

142

of the treacherous verglas. In fact Rudi was happy again, and fell back into his old habits, muttering to himself, cursing the mountain and spurring himself on with encouraging remarks. Where anyone else might have slipped, the guide seemed to fly over the rock-face, without hesitating or stumbling, in a marvellous co-ordination of movement.

After the fissure he attacked the chimney; and twenty minutes later the three friends, trembling with delight, saw Rudi's face grinning at them, bathed in sweat under the hood of the anorak, almost at their feet. Even in the darkness they knew who it was, for he began calling out to them before he reached the traverse itself.

' So there you are, you rascals! A nice way to behave, I must say. Mind you keep still—this is no time to get up to any tricks. I'm coming.'

' Rudi, Rudi, it's you ! ' cried Peter. ' Did you really climb up here on your own ? '

' What about it ? Did you think we'd send a regiment to fetch you ? But there's no time to lose, we can talk when we get down below, and there'll be plenty to say, I promise you. It's a good thing you're not frozen stiff—you've been lucky.'

As he spoke Rudi emptied the rucksack and began helping the children.

# 16

# The Rescue

First of all he made them put on thick pullovers. They did as he told them, numb with cold as they were, clumsy and almost incapable of movement, so that Rudi had to help each one in turn.

Immediately the wind seemed less bitter, and at last they could thrust their blue fingers into warm woolly mitts. Then Rudi took the thermos flasks out of the rucksack and poured them out mugs of scalding hot tea, well sweetened. They drank thirstily, burning their tongues, and the penetrating heat put new heart into them. It was as if the cold dropped from their shoulders, lost its grip on their stiff limbs and left them free once more. The colour gradually returned to their cheeks and a glow of well-being invaded them. Larry would gladly have fallen asleep, but Peter had recovered all his energy.

' It's terrific, Rudi. To climb up alone when it's almost pitch-dark, and with this verglas too ! '

' Just you wait till we're back at the hut—you'll find something else terrific there, I can promise you.'

' But Rudi—it really wasn't our fault—we only . . .'

' We'll see about that. Rest for a little now until you're thawed out and then we'll start off. Hi, Larry, you mustn't go to sleep. It's the worst thing you can do. Drink some more tea—empty the thermos—it'll do you good.'

Peter said no more. He no longer had any doubts about their rescue ; Rudi was there and since he had been able to climb up to them, he would certainly manage to bring them down.

They were warm, they were alive again, and the rest —meaning the welcome awaiting them at the hut— just didn't matter. Peter drank a third mug of tea, stretched his arms and legs and said he was ready.

' Yes, we ought to make haste now,' Rudi agreed. ' We need to lose height as quickly as possible. The tea has done you good, but that won't last long. Come on, stand up. I'll rope you all, and then we'll start.'

Larry and Gretel got up with difficulty. Their joints were painfully stiff and they had to stretch their muscles into play before they were able to move more easily.

The guide explained operations to them. ' I'm going to coil a double loop of rope round this spike. The rappel rope will go through it and you can use it as a hand-rail. You needn't be afraid : you'll be roped and even if you leave go, I shall hold you fast.'

He took up the thick belay rope, knotted a loop round Peter's chest, as he would go down first, paid out a dozen yards or so, knotted another loop for Larry and then one for Gretel, and finally looped the rest firmly round his own chest.

'That's it! We're ready now. Don't move yet, I'm going to fix up the hand-rope.'

He looped a smaller rope twice round the spike, pulled hard at it to test its firmness, passed a double thickness of the rappel rope through the loop and threw it down into space with a sweeping arm movement. It uncoiled completely and struck the rock-face.

'That's fine. Now, Peter, it's up to you.'

'Shall I make a rappel descent?'

'Certainly not! You haven't had enough practice and it would waste time. No, use the rappel rope as a hand-rail and put your feet against the rock, arch your body backwards and let yourself slide down. Do you see, you two? Don't get up to any tricks, this simply isn't the moment. Don't go too fast, so that I can pay out the belay rope. Stop at the overhang on the left at the foot of the chimney. Try to find it. Don't go any lower, the rope might not be long enough. Tuck yourself into the fissure and get hold of Larry when he comes. Do you understand?'

'Right. To the overhang . . '

'And don't worry a bit, I've got you safe.'

Peter checked the knot on his chest, straddled the

146

rappel rope and seized it with both hands, then pressed his feet against the edge of the traverse and leant slowly backwards. Just as he was going to swing himself down he let the rope slide a little through his hands, moved his feet lower down against the rock-face and in this way, using legs and rope alternately, he began the descent.

Rudi crouched under the overhang, his back to the rock, his feet against the spike opposite, and the belay rope passing under his right arm and over his left shoulder. He held the rope tight, paying it out between his hands in little jerks, in time with Peter's descent. Rudi was keeping watch, and Peter was in no danger ; had he let go of the hand-rope the guide would have held him fast, preventing him from falling.

' Do you see how it works ? ' he asked the others. ' It's not really difficult. The chief thing is not to be afraid. Remember, I've got you. It's dark and you can't see, but that doesn't matter. You can still feel the rock. The main thing is to stretch your legs to the full, to hang on tight and to go very slowly.'

' I think I can do it,' said Larry. ' I'm not frightened.'

' What about you, Gretel ? '

' Oh well—I think I shall manage—but it's so cold ! '

' You'll feel better once you start moving. Now, Larry, it's your turn, I think. The rope's gone slack— he must have made it.'

They could hear a faint shout from Peter. He had reached the overhang, more than thirty feet below.

Larry could feel his heart beating loudly : this time he was not climbing for fun, but in deadly earnest. It was pitch dark, there was a strong wind and at his feet yawned a black abyss, but without stopping to wonder whether he was frightened or not, he seized the rappel rope in both hands and swung himself down as Peter had done. He made the right movements instinctively ; it all seemed perfectly straightforward, in spite of the verglas covering the rock-face. Moreover he could feel the pull of the rope round his chest joining him to Rudi, and this gave him a wonderful sense of security ; and from down below he could hear Peter calling to him, cheering him and giving him good advice.

Larry could not really make out what Peter was saying, for the words were lost on the wind, but just to know that his friend was near at hand waiting for him buoyed up his courage, and in a few moments he joined him, everything having gone well. Peter seized him round the waist and hugged him.

' All right, Larry ? You don't feel cold any more ? '

' I'm O.K. My legs still feel a bit stiff and there's a queer buzzing in my ears, but that's nothing.'

Without any more delay, Rudi sent Gretel down to them. Peter climbed up a bit higher inside the fissure to make room for her on the overhang and a second or two later the guide, who had made a rappel descent, joined the three of them.

'Squeeze up a bit. Look out for the verglas, and be careful how you move. We're going on now. The rappel rope is long enough to reach the bottom of the fissure. Things will be easier on the big traverse and we shall be able to breathe. Make room for me inside the chimney so that I can find a solid hold to fix you to. That's it. Now, Peter, start off again, just as you did before.'

They lost no time in carrying out operations along the same lines, but Larry, feeling too sure of himself and scornfully underestimating the difficulties to be reckoned with, went too fast. He slipped on the rock-face, felt himself being thrown backwards and let go, with a loud shriek.

The fall seemed endless, yet it really lasted no more than a fraction of a second, for the safety rope checked it immediately. His right side was brought up sharp against the rock and he let out another yell, which Rudi answered from above with a loud laugh.

'Just look at him swinging like a pendulum ! That'll teach you to try to go too fast. See if you can find the hand-rope again, and be quick about it. I don't want to have to hang on to you much longer—you weigh at least two hundred pounds.'

Larry, wild with fright and scarcely aware of what was happening, spun slowly round at the end of his rope, feeling for the rappel rope in the darkness. His elbow smarted and his thigh was terribly bruised, but he found the rope, seized hold of it with a huge sigh of relief and continued his descent, hardly knowing how he managed it. Peter was waiting to snatch him as he passed and pressed him against the rockface. Then, after announcing his arrival to the others up above, he said to Larry :

' You gave me an awful fright ! What happened ? '

' I don't know. I fell backwards—I dropped down and down—the rope saved me, that's all I remember. But listen, what's that ? '

The guide's voice reached them from up above in a series of hoarse squawks, loud shouts and raucous cries, as if Rudi were being burnt alive.

' That, my dear Larry, is Rudi singing. Haven't you ever heard him giving tongue ? Well, now's your chance. It sounds as if he's thoroughly happy.'

Rudi was indeed happy. His heart was full of joy, for all his troubles were over. The mountain was his friend again. He felt a lump come into his throat and his eyes almost filled with tears, so great was his relief ; and when he joined the three young people, after a steep rappel descent, he gave full rein to his gladness by uttering a resounding yodel which must surely have brought the good tidings to the Schneehorn hut. Then he slipped the rappel rope along by pulling on one of the ends.

' It will be better when we're off the traverse, chaps !
When we reach the dihedral there won't be any more
verglas. You'll only have to slide down on your
behinds and you'll soon reach the bottom.'

It seemed less cold to them now ; they had come a
long way down and the wind blew less strongly,
broken as it was by the couloir. Rudi set up the rappel
twice more—above the dihedral, and for descending
the slab. Eventually, without any more accidents,
all four reached the glacier. They stayed roped together as far as the foot of the moraine, and twenty
minutes later they reached the hut.

The heat inside nearly suffocated them. They pulled
off their jerseys, and then the reaction came.

They had been rescued, and they had returned safe
and sound to the hut, the familiar hut which seemed
lovelier than the most luxurious hotel. While they
were still struggling there had been no time to think,
but now everything hit them at once—fear, relief,
panic, the whole sum of the anguish they had been
through, and they trembled with the excitement of
it all.

Father Rödli's welcome, however, was certainly
calculated to calm them down. The walls of the hut
had never heard anything like it : it was a perfect
disgrace, such asinine behaviour was absolutely un-
paralleled, there never were such crazy lunatics.
He longed to give all three a good beating, beginning

with Peter, and he didn't want them around the hut a moment longer. They could have no idea of how stupid they had been or how mad it was to risk other people's lives. As for them, who cared, but what about those who had to rescue them ? Had they thought about that ? If they hadn't even the smallest grain of sense they'd much better stay down in the valley.

Rudi was laughing at the top of his voice, the children were all talking at the same time, trying to make excuses for themselves, while Father Rödli went on scolding them. The din was terrific.

' Stop it, Rödli ! ' shouted Rudi. ' Let's call a truce ! All's well that ends well. They're back safe and sound and that's all that matters. These things happen in life and it will be a lesson to them. Bring us some tea, and something to eat ! '

When the three friends, after eating their fill and drinking mugs of hot tea, had fallen asleep, at the end of their tether, Rudi told the keeper the whole story. And late into the night, while a howling wind tore to shreds the mist rising from the valley, Rudi Saax laid his plans for the future.

## 17

## The End of the Holiday

The following morning, Father Rödli would gladly
have sent the three 'heroes' back to the valley; he
never wished to live again through the suspense of the
evening before, and, as he said, 'These lunatics are
capable of anything and everything, unless we tie them
up.'

But luck was on their side once more : the hut was
veiled in mist and a fine rain was falling. Bad weather
had come with a vengeance, and Father Rödli had not
the heart to send them out into it.

'It doesn't matter. You'll gain nothing by waiting,
for as soon as it clears, I'll send you packing.'

As for Rudi, nothing could hold him. At daybreak,
without even waiting to drink a bowl of tea, he started
for the valley with the speed of a madman. Rödli
insisted on accompanying him to the foot of the
moraine, and when the two men took leave of each
other they shook hands warmly. No words were
necessary, they understood each other perfectly.

The guide was radiant. His hair bristled, his eyes

shone and he beamed with joy ; he was once more
the man he used to be, whom Rödli knew so well.
Long after Rudi had vanished into the mist, which
quickly swallowed him up, the keeper heard his gay
yodels echoing over the mountains.

Rödli made his way slowly back to the hut, feeling
very happy, not only because the children were safe
but also because Rudi was himself again.

Even if he had wanted to, the keeper could not have
sent his visitors away. It rained for three whole days and
he was really very pleased to have them. They kept him
company, saving him from the loneliness that was often
hard to bear, and they brought life and movement into
the hut, which now became their domain. The place
rang with songs and laughter, stampedes through the
dormitories and noisy games, and in the evenings,
when they gathered round the solitary lamp, Father
Rödli told them all the mountain stories he knew.

Naturally they talked about Rudi too.

' Do you believe that chamois story, Godfather ?
As if Rudi would be frightened of a chamois ! '

' There's no knowing—strange things happen in the
mountains, that can't always be explained away. All
things are possible, you know. But I think it's more
likely that Rudi had a shock. A fall like the one he
had last year is something to reckon with, I can tell
you. It makes a deep impression, and it took away
his faith in himself, so that when he tried to climb he

was lost as soon as he touched the rock-face. Georg ought to have taken him in tow—but Rudi never said anything to anyone, he's so stubborn.'

' But then how did he manage to rescue us ? '

' Oh, that was different. That was just what he needed. He knew that he *had* to do it—and he climbed superbly. In fact . . .'

' In fact we did him a service without knowing it ! '

' That's one way of looking at it ! But do you realise what would have happened, Peter, if he hadn't suc-ceeded ? He would have fallen, while as for you three . . . Let it be a lesson to you. For a future guide it seems to me you're pretty scatter-brained, my boy.'

Peter was forced to hang his head. He was in fact deeply ashamed, and swore to himself that nothing like that would ever happen again ; he realised perfectly that the results might have been disastrous. On the mountain heights, rashness, carelessness and conceit are inexcusable, as Peter ought to have known, and the consciousness of his lapse spoilt his stay at the hut.

On the fourth morning he was glad to see that the weather had changed. Father Rödli had already forecast this the evening before ; the wind had veered and in the early part of the night they glimpsed several stars between the trails of mist.

As the morning wore on the sky cleared and the last clouds vanished. Towards noon the day became

156

brilliantly fine, and it was settled that the two boys should start off after lunch. Gretel was to stay on for a few days. ' When those two dare-devils have gone I shan't worry,' Father Rödli said. ' You won't get up to any tricks on your own.'

Gretel kissed him on both cheeks. She wasn't deceived and knew perfectly well that her grandfather didn't want her to go back to Frutigen yet.

They exchanged heartfelt goodbyes and Larry promised to come up again the following year; they all swore not to forget each other, but always to remember the wonderful time they had spent together. Heavy-hearted, the two boys began the descent, with a last look at the Schneehorn rock-face which had nearly cost them their lives.

Gretel and her grandfather stood waving farewell from the foot of the moraine, then they were lost to sight. The boys walked fast without speaking, feeling sad. Their adventure was over, and for Larry it was almost the end of his holidays too. His parents awaited him at the Grubers' house, and in a few days they would be returning home.

Towards four o'clock they reached the falls above the lake and paused for a breather. High up above them, a tiny speck in its magnificent frame at the foot of the Schneehorn mountain, they could just discern the hut. Larry's heart was torn at the thought of leaving the mountains, but he swore to himself that he

would soon be back and that his first trip would be to
visit the Schneehorn hut and Father Rödli.

' Look, Larry, there's a party coming up.  As soon
as the weather's fine they're off again—they don't
lose much time.'

Three men were climbing the path just below them
and to their surprise they saw that the leader was
Rudi.

The two boys got to their feet in one bound and
rushed to meet him.  Rudi, seeing them coming,
burst out laughing.

' Well, boys, you seem in a great hurry.  Steady on !
Has Rödli thrown you out on your ear ? '

' Rudi, Rudi !  It's you ! '

' Why not—what's so strange about that ?  I've got
two clients who want to climb the Galletgrat, so . . .'

' You're going up there ?  That's terrific ! '

' It's all in the day's work—it's my job, isn't it ? '

Rudi looked splendid, freshly equipped in handsome
trousers, a new rucksack and a bright red shirt such as
only Rudi could wear.  Peter felt rather embarrassed :
he would have liked to thank the guide, but didn't
know how to set about it.

' Listen, Rudi.  I wanted . . . to tell you . . .'

' That's all right !  One of these days when I've
time I'll climb up to the Golitschen and give you a
good hiding—then we'll be quits ! '

He gave him a friendly dig in the ribs and was about

to start on his way again when he added : ' One other thing. Don't worry any more about the chamois—that chapter's closed.'

He gave a loud laugh, the hearty laugh of a man entirely sure of himself, which was so infectious that everyone joined in. Then the two little groups parted company. A bit higher up Rudi stopped once more and called out through his cupped hands :

' Hi there, Peter ! '

' Yes, Rudi ? '

' I'll get in touch with you one of these days, and we'll climb the Schneehorn together to make up for the dance you led me the other day ! '

Peter was dumbfounded with joy and astonishment. To climb the Schneehorn roped together with Rudi ! It was the most wonderful thing that could happen to him.

The two boys stayed there for a long time, gazing after the three diminishing silhouettes approaching the top of the gully. Their thoughts went out to their friend Rudi, who with recovered zest and freedom of heart was embarking on a new round of adventure in the midst of his mountain kingdom. And as if in a dream Larry seemed to see, far away on the Golit-schengrat, another creature in love with space and solitude—the chamois, proud and free, a king among the mountain peaks.

# Glossary

| | |
|---|---|
| *Belay* | Make fast by hitching rope to projection and passing it round body |
| *Chimney* | Steep narrow cleft in rock or ice |
| *Couloir* | Wide steep gulley |
| *Crampon* | Steel spikes on frame, fixed to boot for use on ice |
| *Crevasse* | Fissure in glacier or snowfield |
| *Dihedral* | Two rock walls at angles, like an open book |
| *Foehn* | Warm south wind, generally signalling bad weather |
| *Gendarme* | Rock-tower on mountain ridge |
| *Moraine* | Rock and debris brought down by glacier |
| *Piton* | Steel spike, ringed at the end, which can be driven into rock or ice to support hand, foot or rope |
| *Rappel* | Descent of steep slope by means of doubled rope |
| *Rimaye* | Crevasse in glacier |
| *Sérac* | Ice-pinnacle found in glaciers |
| *Traverse* | Horizontal or diagonal crossing of mountain-side |
| *Verglas* | Thin coating of ice on rock, very tough and treacherous |